Best in Children's Books

Copyright ©, 1959, by Nelson Doubleday, Inc.
Garden City, New York   23

Ali Baba and the Forty Thieves

illustrated by
FEODOR
ROJANKOVSKY

In a town in Persia lived two brothers named Cassim and Ali Baba. Their father at his death had left what little property he possessed divided equally between them. Cassim, however, having married the heiress of a rich merchant, became soon after his marriage the owner of a fine shop, together with several pieces of land, and was in consequence, through no effort of his own, the wealthiest merchant in the town. Ali Baba, on the other hand, was married to one as poor as himself, and having no other means of gaining a livelihood he used to go every day into the forest to cut wood. Loading the three asses which were his sole stock-in-trade, he would then hawk the wood about the streets for sale.

One day while he was at work in the forest, Ali Baba saw, advancing towards him across the open, a large company of horsemen. Fearing from their appearance that they might be robbers, he left his asses to their own devices and sought safety for himself in the lower branches of a large tree

Text adapted from *Stories from the Arabian Nights*, retold by Lawrence Housman, and published by Jonathan Cape Limited.

1

which grew beside a towering wall of rock.

Almost immediately it became evident that this very rock was the goal toward which the troop was bound. For having arrived they alighted instantly from their horses, and took down—each man of them—a sack which seemed by its weight and form to be filled with gold. There could no longer be any doubt that they were robbers. Ali Baba counted forty of them.

Just then the one nearest to him, who seemed to be their chief, advanced toward the rock, and in a low but distinct voice uttered the two words, "Open, Sesamé!" Immediately the rock opened like a door, the captain and his men passed in, and the rock closed behind them.

2

For a long while Ali Baba waited, not daring to descend from his hiding place lest they should come out and find him watching; but at last, when the waiting had grown almost unbearable, his patience was rewarded. The door in the rock opened, and out came the forty men, their captain leading them. When the last of them was through, "Shut, Sesamé!" said the captain, and immediately the face of the rock closed together as before. Then they all mounted their horses and rode away.

As soon as he felt sure that they were not returning, Ali Baba came down from the tree and made his way at once to that part of the rock where he had seen the captain and his men enter. And there at the words "Open, Sesamé!" a door suddenly revealed itself and opened.

Ali Baba had expected to find a dark and gloomy cavern. Great was his astonishment therefore when he perceived a spacious and vaulted chamber lighted from above through a fissure in the rock. And there spread out before him lay treasures in profusion: bales of merchandise, silks, carpets, brocades, and—above all—gold, jewels, and silver lying in loose heaps or in sacks piled one upon another. He did not

take long to consider what he should do. Disregarding the
silver, the jewels, and the gold that lay loose, he brought to
the mouth of the cave as many sacks of gold as he thought
his three asses might carry; and having loaded them on and
covered them with wood so that they might not be seen, he
closed the rock by the utterance of the magic words which
he had learned, and departed for the town, a well-satisfied
man.

5

When he got home he drove his asses into a small court,
and shutting the gates carefully he took off the wood that
covered the bags and carried the bags to his wife. She, dis-
covering them to be full of gold, feared that her husband
had stolen them, and began sorrowfully to reproach him.
But Ali Baba soon put her mind at rest on that score; and
having poured all the gold into a great heap upon the floor,

he sat down at her side to consider how well it looked.

Soon his wife, poor careful body, must needs begin counting it over piece by piece. Ali Baba let her go on for awhile, but before long the sight set him laughing. "Wife," said he, "you will never make an end of it that way. The best thing to do is to dig a hole and bury it, then we shall be sure that it is not slipping through our fingers."

"That will do well enough," said his wife, "but it would be better first to have the measure of it. So while you dig the hole I will go round to Cassim's and borrow a measure small enough to give us an exact reckoning."

"Do as you will," answered her husband, "but see that you keep the thing secret."

Off went Ali Baba's wife to her brother-in-law's house. Cassim was away from home, so she begged of his wife the loan of a small measure, naming for choice the smallest. This set the sister-in-law wondering. Knowing Ali Baba's poverty, she was all the more curious to find out for what kind of grain so small a measure could be needed. So before bringing it she covered all the bottom with lard, and giving it to Ali Baba's wife told her to be sure and be quick in returning it. The other, promising to restore it punctually, made haste to get home; and there finding the hole dug for the treasure, she started to measure the money into it. First she set the measure upon the heap, then she filled it, then she carried it to the hole; and so she continued till the last measure was counted. Then, leaving Ali Baba to finish the burying, she carried back the measure with all haste to her sister-in-law, returning thanks for the loan.

No sooner was her back turned than Cassim's wife

looked at the bottom of the measure, and there to her astonishment she saw sticking to the lard a gold coin. "What?" she cried, her heart filled with envy, "is Ali Baba so rich that he needs a measure for his gold? Where, then, I would know, has the miserable wretch obtained it?"

She waited with impatience for her husband's return, and as soon as he came in she began to jeer at him. "You think yourself rich," said she, "but Ali Baba is richer. You count your gold by the piece, but Ali Baba does not count, he measures it! In comparison to Ali Baba we are but grubs and groundlings!"

Having thus ridiculed him in order to provoke his curiosity, she told him the story of the borrowed measure, of her own stratagem, and of its result.

Cassim, instead of being pleased at Ali Baba's sudden prosperity, grew furiously jealous; not a wink could he sleep all night for thinking of it. The next morning before sunrise he went to his brother's house. "Ali Baba," said he, "what do you mean by pretending to be poor, when all the time you are scooping up gold by the quart?"

"Brother," said Ali Baba, "explain your meaning."

"My meaning shall be plain!" cried Cassim, displaying the telltale coin. "How many more pieces have you, like this that my wife found sticking to the bottom of the measure yesterday?"

Ali Baba, realizing that the interference of the wives had

made further concealment useless, told his brother the true facts of the case, and offered him, as an inducement for keeping the secret, an equal share of the treasure.

"That is the least that I have the right to expect," answered Cassim haughtily. "It is further necessary that you tell me exactly where the treasure lies, that I may, if need be, test the truth of your story. Otherwise I shall find it my duty to denounce you to the authorities."

Ali Baba, having a clear conscience, had little fear of Cassim's threats; but out of pure good nature he gave him all the information he desired, not forgetting to instruct him in the words which would give him free passage into the cave and out again.

Cassim, who was intent on possessing himself of all the treasures which yet remained, set off the next morning before daybreak, taking with him ten mules laden with empty crates. Having arrived before the cave, he recalled the words which his brother had taught him. No sooner was "Open, Sesamé!" said than the door in the rock lay wide for him to pass through, and when he had entered it shut again.

If the simple soul of Ali Baba had found delight in the riches of the cavern, greater still was the exultation of a greedy nature like Cassim's. Intoxicated with the wealth that lay before his eyes, he had no thought but to gather together with all speed as much treasure as the ten mules could carry; and so, having exhausted himself with heavy labor and avaricious excitement, he suddenly found on returning to the door that he had forgotten the key which opened it. Up and down, and in and out through his brain he chased the missing word. Barley and maize and rice—he thought of them all. But of sesamé never once, because his mind had become dark to the revealing light of heaven. And so the door stayed fast, holding him prisoner in the cave, where to his fate, undeserving of pity, we leave him.

Toward noon the robbers returned, and saw, standing about the rock, the ten mules laden with crates. At this they were greatly surprised, and began to search with suspi-

cion amongst the surrounding crannies and undergrowth. Finding no one there, they drew their swords and advanced cautiously toward the cave, where, upon the captain's pronouncement of the magic word, the door immediately fell open. Cassim, who from within could hear the trampling of horses, doubted not that the robbers had returned and that his last hour had come. Resolved however to make one desperate effort at escape, he stood ready by the door; and no sooner had the opening word been uttered than he sprang forth with such violence that he threw the captain to the ground. But his attempt was vain; before he could break through he was mercilessly hacked down by the swords of the robber band.

Now the robbers anxiously entered the cave to view the traces of its late visitor. There they saw piled by the door the treasure which Cassim had sought to carry away; but while restoring this to its place they failed altogether to notice the earlier loss which Ali Baba had caused them. Reckoning, however, that as one had discovered the secret of entry others also might know of it, they determined to leave an example for any who might venture thither on a similar errand. They set the body of Cassim at the entrance in a manner that could not fail to strike horror into the heart of the beholder. Then, closing the door of the cave, they rode away in search of more plunder.

Meanwhile Cassim's wife had grown very uneasy at her husband's long absence; and at nightfall, unable to endure further suspense, she ran to Ali Baba. Telling him of his brother's secret expedition, she entreated him to go out instantly in search of him.

Ali Baba had too kind a heart to refuse. Taking with him

his three asses he set out immediately for the forest, and as the road was familiar to him he had soon found his way to the door of the cave. When he saw there the traces of blood he became filled with misgiving, but no sooner had he entered than his worst fears were realized. Nevertheless he wrapped his brother's body with all possible decency, and laid it upon one of the asses. Then thinking that he deserved some payment for his pains, he loaded the two remaining asses with sacks of gold, and covering them with wood as on the first occasion, made his way back to the town while it was yet early. Leaving his wife to dispose of the treasure borne by the two asses, he led the third to his sister-in-law's house, and knocking quietly so that none of the neighbors might hear, was presently admitted by Morgiana, a female slave whose intelligence and discretion had long been known to him. "Morgiana," said he, "there's trouble on the back of that ass. Can you keep a secret?" And Morgiana's nod satisfied him better than any oath. "Well," said he, "your master's body lies there, and our business now is to bury him honorably as though he had

died a natural death. Go and tell your mistress that I want to speak to her."

Morgiana went in to her mistress, and returning presently bade Ali Baba enter. Then, leaving him to break to his sister-in-law the news and the sad circumstances of his brother's death, she, with her plan already formed, hastened forth to the nearest apothecary. As soon as he opened the door, Morgiana demanded certain pills, declaring in answer to his questions that her master had been taken suddenly ill. With these pills she returned home. And her plan having been explained and agreed upon much to the satisfaction of Ali Baba, she went forth the next morning to the same apothecary, and with tears in her eyes besought him to supply her in haste with a certain drug that is given to sick people only in the last extremity. Meanwhile the rumor of Cassim's sickness had got abroad. Ali Baba and his wife had been seen coming and going, while Morgiana by her ceaseless activity had made the two days' pretended illness seem like a fortnight: so when a sound of wailing arose within the house all the neighbors concluded without

further question that Cassim had died a natural and honorable death.

But Morgiana had now a still more difficult task to perform: the body must be made in some way presentable for the funeral. So at a very early hour the next morning she went to the shop of a certain merry old tailor, Baba Mustapha by name, who lived on the other side of the town. Showing him a piece of gold she inquired whether he were ready to earn it by doing exactly as she told him. When Baba Mustapha sought to know the terms, Morgiana said, "First you must come with your eyes bandaged; second, you must sew what I put before you without asking questions; and third, when you return you must tell nobody."

Mustapha, who had a lively curiosity, nevertheless promised secrecy readily enough—for double the fee. And taking his tailor's tools in hand, submitted himself to Morgiana's guidance and set forth. This way and that she led him blindfold, till she had brought him to the house of her deceased master. Then, uncovering his eyes in the presence of the corpse, she bade him get out thread and sew a burial robe close about Cassim's body to conceal the wounds made by the robbers.

Baba Mustapha plied his task according to the agreement, asking no question. When he had done, Morgiana again bandaged his eyes and led him home. And giving him a third piece of gold the more to satisfy him, she bade him good day and departed.

So without scandal of any kind the funeral rites of the murdered Cassim were performed. And when all was ended, Ali Baba moved with all his goods and newly ac-

quired treasure to the house which had been his brother's.
And having also acquired the shop where Cassim had done
business, he put into it his own son, who had already served
an apprenticeship to the trade. So, with his fortune well
established, let us now leave Ali Baba and return to the
robbers' cave.

Thither, at the appointed time, came the forty robbers,
bearing in hand fresh booty; and great was their dismay to
discover that not only had the body of Cassim been removed, but a good many sacks of gold as well. It was no
wonder that this should trouble them, for so long as any
one could enter it secretly, the cave was useless as a hiding
place for their wealth. The question was: What could they
do to put an end to this state of affairs? After long debate,
it was agreed that one of their number should go into the

town disguised as a traveler, and there, mixing with the common people, learn from their gossip whether there had been recently any case in their midst of sudden prosperity or sudden death. If such a thing could be discovered, then they would be sure they could track their trouble to its source and find a remedy.

Although the penalty for failure was death, one of the robbers at once boldly offered himself for the venture, and having transformed himself by disguise, he set out for the town.

Arriving at dawn, he began to walk up and down the streets and watch the early stirring of the inhabitants. Before long he drew up at the door of Baba Mustapha, who, though old, was already seated at work upon his tailor's

bench. The robber accosted him. "I wonder," said he, "to
see a man of your age at work so early. Does not so dull a
light strain your eyes?"

"Not so much as you might think," answered Baba Mustapha. "Why, it was but the other day that at this same
hour I saw well enough to stitch a burial robe on a wounded
body in a place where it was certainly no lighter."

"Stitch a robe on a wounded body!" cried the robber, in
pretended amazement, concealing his joy at this sudden
intelligence. "Surely you cannot mean that some family
wished to conceal a violent death!"

"What I say I mean," said Mustapha. "But as it is a
secret, I can tell you no more."

The robber drew out a piece of gold. "Come," said he, "tell me nothing you do not care to; only show me the house where lay the body that you thus concealed."

Baba Mustapha eyed the gold longingly. "Would that I could," he replied; "but alas! I went to it blindfold."

"Well," said the robber, "I have heard that a blind man remembers his road. Perhaps, though seeing it you might lose it, blindfold you might find it again."

Tempted by the offer of a second piece of gold, Baba Mustapha was soon persuaded to make the attempt. "It was here that I started," said he, showing the spot, "and I turned as you see me now." The robber then put a bandage over his eyes, and walked beside him through the streets, partly guiding and partly being led, till of his own accord Baba Mustapha stopped. "It was here," said he. "The door by which I went in should now lie to the right." And he had in fact come exactly opposite to the house which had once been Cassim's where Ali Baba now dwelt.

The robber marked the door with a piece of chalk which he had provided for the purpose, and returned with all possible speed to the cave where his comrades were awaiting him.

Soon after, Morgiana happened to go out upon an errand, and as she returned she noticed the mark upon the door. "This," she thought, "is not as it should be; either some trick is intended, or there is evil brewing for my master's house." Taking a piece of chalk she put a similar mark upon the five or six doors lying to right and left; and having done this she went home with her mind satisfied, saying nothing.

In the meantime the robbers had learned from their companion the success of his venture. Greatly elated at the thought of the vengeance so soon to be theirs, they formed a plan for entering the city in a manner that should arouse no suspicion among the inhabitants. Passing in by twos and threes, and by different routes, they came together to the market place at an appointed time, while the captain and the robber who had acted as spy made their way alone to the street in which the marked door was to be found. Presently, just as they had expected, they perceived a door with the mark on it. "That is it!" said the robber. But as they continued walking so as to avoid suspicion, they came upon another and another, till, before they were done, they had passed six in succession. So alike were the marks that the spy, though he swore he had made but one, could not tell which it was. Seeing that the plot had failed, the captain returned to the market place, and having passed the word for his troop to go back in the same way as they had come, he himself left the town.

When they were all reassembled in the forest, the spy submitted to his fate, kneeled down, and received the stroke of the executioner.

But as it was still necessary for the safety of all that so great a theft should not pass unavenged, another of the band, despite the fate of his comrade, volunteered upon the same conditions to carry on the search. Coming by the same means to the house of Ali Baba, he set upon the door, at a spot not likely to be noticed, a mark in red chalk to distinguish it clearly from those which were already marked in white. But even this failed. Morgiana, whose eye nothing could escape, noticed the red mark at the first time of passing, and dealt with it just as she had done with the previous one. So when all the robbers came, hoping this time to light upon the door without fail, they found not one but six all similarly marked with red.

When the second spy had been executed, the captain considered how by relying on others he had come to lose two of his bravest followers. So the third attempt he determined to conduct in person. Having found his way to Ali Baba's door, as the two others had done by the aid of Baba

Mustapha, he did not set any mark upon it, but examined it so carefully that he could not in future mistake it. He then returned to the forest and explained to his band the plan which he had formed. This was to go into the town in the disguise of an oil merchant, bearing with him upon nineteen mules thirty-eight large leather jars, one of which, as a sample, was to be full of oil, but all the others empty. In these jars he intended to conceal the thirty-seven robbers (to which his band was now reduced), and thus to transport them to the house of Ali Baba.

Within a couple of days he had secured all the mules and jars that were needed. And having hidden the thirty-seven robbers in the oil jars, he drove his train of well-laden mules to the gates of the city, through which he passed just before sunset. Proceeding thence to Ali Baba's house, and arriving as it fell dark, he perceived Ali Baba at the door enjoying the fresh air after supper. Addressing him in tones of respect he said, "Sir, I have brought my oil a great distance to sell tomorrow in the market; and at this late hour, be-

ing a stranger, I know not where to seek for a shelter. If it is not troubling you too much, allow me to stable my beasts here for the night."

The captain's voice was now so changed from its accustomed tone of command, that Ali Baba, though he had heard it before, did not recognize it. Not only did he grant the stranger's request, but as soon as the unloading and stabling of the mules had been accomplished, he invited him to enter the house as his guest. The captain, afraid that his plan might go awry, tried to excuse himself. But since Ali Baba would take no refusal he was forced at last to submit with apparent cheerfulness to an entertainment which the hospitality of his host extended to a late hour.

When they were about to retire for the night, Ali Baba went into the kitchen to speak to Morgiana; and the captain of the robbers, on the pretext of going to look after his mules, slipped out into the yard where the oil jars were standing in line. Passing from jar to jar he whispered into each, "When you hear a handful of pebbles fall from the window of the chamber where I am lodged, then cut your way out of the jar and make ready, for the time will have come." He then returned to the house, where Morgiana came with a light and conducted him to his chamber.

Now Ali Baba, before going to bed, had said to Morgiana, "Tomorrow at dawn I am going to the baths; let my bath linen be put ready, and see that the cook has some good broth prepared for me against my return." Having therefore led the guest up to his chamber, Morgiana returned to the kitchen and ordered Abdallah the cook to

put on the pot for the broth. Suddenly while she was skimming it, the lamp went out, and, on searching, she found there was no more oil in the house. At so late an hour no shop would be open, yet somehow the broth had to be made, and that could not be done without a light.

"As for that," said Abdallah, seeing her perplexity, "why trouble yourself? There is plenty of oil out in the yard."

"Why, to be sure!" said Morgiana, and sending Abdallah to bed so that he might be up in time to wake his master on the morrow, she took the oil can herself and went out into the court. As she approached the jar which stood nearest, she heard a voice within say, "Is it time?"

To one of Morgiana's intelligence an oil jar that spoke was an object of even more suspicion than a chalk mark on a door, and in an instant she realized what danger for her master and his family might lie concealed around her.

Understanding well enough that an oil jar which asked a question required an answer, she replied quick as thought, "Not yet, but presently." And thus she passed from jar to jar, thirty-seven in all, giving the same answer, till she came to the one which contained the oil.

The situation was now clear to her. Aware of the source from which her master had acquired his wealth, she guessed at once that, in extending shelter to the oil merchant, Ali Baba had in fact admitted to his house the robber captain and his band. On the instant her resolution was formed. Having filled the oil can she returned to the kitchen. There she lighted the lamp, and then, taking a large kettle, went back once more to the jar which contained the oil. Filling the kettle she carried it back to the kitchen and, putting under it a great fire of wood, soon brought it to the boil. Then taking it in hand once more, she went out into the yard and poured into each jar in turn a sufficient quantity of the boiling oil to scald its occupant to death.

She then returned to the kitchen, and having made Ali Baba's broth, put out the fire, blew out the lamp, and sat down by the window to watch.

Before long the captain of the robbers awoke from the short sleep which he had allowed himself, and finding that all was silent in the house, he rose softly and opened the window. Below stood the oil jars; gently into their midst he threw the handful of pebbles agreed on as a signal; but from the oil jars came no answer. He threw a second and a third time; yet though he could hear the pebbles falling among the jars, there followed only the silence of the dead. Wondering whether his band had fled leaving him in the lurch, or whether they were all asleep, he grew uneasy, and descending in haste, made his way into the court. As he approached the first jar a smell of burning oil assailed his nostrils, and looking within he beheld the dead body of his comrade. In every jar the same sight presented itself till he came to the one which had contained the oil. There, in what was missing, the means and manner of his companions' death were made clear to him. Aghast at the discovery and awake to the danger that now threatened him, he did not delay an instant, but forcing the garden gate, and thence climbing from wall to wall, he made his escape out of the city.

When Morgiana, who had remained all this time on the watch, was assured of his final departure, she put her master's bath linen ready, and went to bed well satisfied with her day's work.

The next morning Ali Baba, awakened by his slave, went to the baths before daybreak. On his return he was greatly surprised to find that the merchant was gone, leaving his mules and oil jars behind him. He inquired of Morgiana the reason. "You will find the reason," said she, "if you look into the first jar you come to." Ali Baba did so, and, seeing a man, started back with a cry.

"Do not be afraid," said Morgiana, "he is dead and harmless; and so are all the others whom you will find if you look further."

As Ali Baba went from one jar to another finding always the same sight of horror within, his knees trembled under him; and when he came at last to the one empty oil jar, he stood for a time motionless, turning upon Morgiana eyes

of wonder and inquiry. "And what," he said then, "has become of the merchant?"

Morgiana gave him the whole history, so far as she knew it, from beginning to end; and by her intelligent explanation left him at last in no possible doubt as to the nature of the plot which her quick wits had so happily defeated. "And now, dear master," she said in conclusion, "continue to be on your guard, for though all these are dead, one remains alive; and he, if I mistake not, is the captain of the band, and for that reason the one most to be dreaded."

When Morgiana had done speaking, Ali Baba clearly perceived that he owed her his life. With his heart full of gratitude, he said, "I will reward you as you deserve; from this moment I give you your liberty."

This token of his approval filled Morgiana's heart with delight, although she had no intention of leaving so kind a master. The immediate question, she felt, was how to dispose of the bodies. Luckily at the far end of the garden stood a thick grove of trees, and under these Ali Baba was able to dig a large trench without attracting the notice of his neighbors. Here the thirty-seven robbers were laid side by side, the trench was filled again, and the ground made level. As for the mules, since Ali Baba had no use for them, he sent them, one or two at a time, to the market to be sold.

Meanwhile the robber captain had fled back to the forest. Entering the cave he was overcome by its gloom and loneliness. "Alas!" he cried, "my comrades, partners in my adventures, sharers of my fortune, how shall I endure to live without you? Why did I lead you to such a fate? Surely had you died sword in hand my sorrow had been less bitter! Now nothing remains for me but to take vengeance for your death!"

Thus resolved, at an early hour the next day he assumed a disguise, and going to the town took lodging at an inn. Entering into conversation with his host, he inquired whether anything of interest had happened recently in the town; but the other, though full of gossip, had heard nothing of the affair at the house of Ali Baba.

The captain then inquired where there was a shop for

hire; and hearing of one that suited him, he came to terms with the owner, and before long had furnished it with all kinds of rich stuffs and carpets and jewelry which he brought by degrees with great secrecy from the cave.

Now this shop happened to be opposite to that which had belonged to Cassim and was now occupied by the son of Ali Baba; so before long the son and the newcomer, who had taken the name of Cogia Houssain, became close friends.

Cogia Houssain did all he could to further this false friendship, for he had soon learned how the young man and Ali Baba were related. And before many days he found himself invited to sup at the house of Ali Baba. The

robber captain, though delighted that his plan was moving ahead so swiftly, pretended reluctance. But the son conducted him to his father's door, and Ali Baba himself, coming to meet them, urged them in the most kindly manner to enter. Here they found the table set and the food prepared.

But now an unlooked-for difficulty arose. Wicked though he might be, the robber captain was not so impious a Moslem as to eat the salt of the man he intended to kill. He therefore began with many apologies to excuse himself; and when Ali Baba sought to know the reason, the robber captain said, "Sir, I have made it a rule to eat of no dish that has salt in it. How then can I sit down at your table if I must reject everything that is set before me?"

"If that is your scruple," said Ali Baba, "it shall soon be satisfied." And he sent orders to the kitchen that no salt was to be put into any of the dishes presently to be served to the newly arrived guest. "Thus," said he to Cogia Houssain, "I shall still have the honor, to which I have looked forward, of returning to you under my own roof the hospitality you have shown to my son."

Morgiana, who was just about to serve supper, received the order with astonishment. "Who," she said, "is this difficult person that refuses to eat salt? He must be a curiosity worth looking at." So when the saltless courses were ready to be set upon the table, she herself helped to carry in the dishes. No sooner had she set eyes on Cogia Houssain than she recognized him in spite of his disguise; and observing his movements with great attention she saw that he had a dagger concealed beneath his robe. "Ah!"

31

she said to herself, "here is reason enough! For who will eat salt with the man he means to murder? But he shall not murder my master if I can prevent it."

Now Morgiana knew that the most favorable time for the robber captain to carry out his design would be at the end of the meal, when Ali Baba and his son and guest were alone together over their wine (which indeed was the very scheme that Cogia Houssain had in mind). Going forth, therefore, in haste, she dressed herself as a dancer, assuming a headdress and mask. Then she fastened a silver girdle about her waist, and hung upon it a dagger of the same material. Thus equipped, she said to Abdallah the cook, "Take your tabor and let us go in and give an entertainment in honor of our master's guest."

So Abdallah took his tabor, and played Morgiana into the hall. As soon as she had entered she made a low curtsey, and stood awaiting orders. Then Ali Baba, seeing that she wished to perform for his guest, said kindly, "Come in, Morgiana, and show Cogia Houssain what you can do."

Immediately, Abdallah began to beat upon his tabor and sing an air; and Morgiana, advancing with much grace, began to move through the complicated figures of a dance, with ease and dexterity. Then, for the last figure of all, she drew out the dagger and, holding it in her hand, danced a dance which excelled all that had preceded it in the

surprise and quickness of its movements. Now she presented the dagger at her own breast, now at one of the onlookers, as though this were part of the action. At length, she snatched Abdallah's tabor from him with her left hand, and, still holding the dagger in her right, advanced the hollow of the tabor toward her master, as is the custom of dancers when claiming their fee. Ali Baba threw in a piece of gold; his son did likewise. Then advancing it in the same manner toward Cogia Houssain, who was feeling for his purse, she struck with her right hand, and before he knew it, had plunged her dagger deep into his heart.

Ali Baba and his son, seeing their guest fall dead, cried

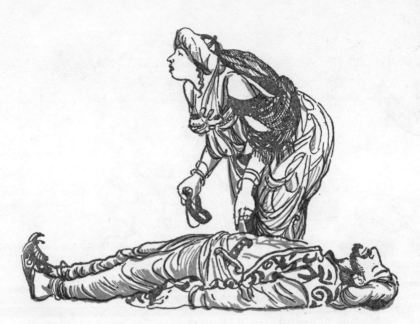

out in horror, "What ruin and shame hast thou brought on us?"

"Nay," answered Morgiana, "it is not your ruin but your life that I have thus secured. Look and see this enemy who refused to eat salt with you!" So saying, she tore off the dead robber's disguise, showing the concealed dagger and the face which her master now for the first time recognized.

Ali Baba's gratitude to Morgiana, for thus preserving his life a second time, knew no bounds. He took her in his arms and embraced her as a daughter. "Now," said he, "the time is come when I must fulfill my debt; and how better can I do it than by marrying you to my son?"

To this proposal the young man joyously consented, and a few days later the nuptials were celebrated with great splendor. The marriage thus auspiciously begun yielded as much happiness as lies within the power of mortals to secure.

As for the robbers' cave, it remained the secret possession of Ali Baba and his family. And using their good fortune with justice and moderation, they rose to high office in the city and were held in great honor by all who knew them.

Tom, the Piper's Son

*With all the fun
That he has done*

an old nursery rhyme

illustrated by
ROBERTA MACDONALD

Tom, he was a piper's son,
He learned to play when he was young,
But all the tune that he could play
Was "Over the hills and far away."
Over the hills and a great way off,
The wind shall blow my top-knot off.

Tom with his pipe made such a noise,
That he pleased both the girls and boys;
They all danced while he did play
"Over the hills and far away."
   Over the hills and a great way off,
   The wind shall blow my top-knot off.

Tom with his pipe did play with such skill
That those who heard him could never keep still;
As soon as he played they began for to dance,
Even pigs on their hind legs would after him prance.
Over the hills and a great way off,
The wind shall blow my top-knot off.

As Dolly was milking her cow one day,
Tom took his pipe and began for to play;
So Doll and the cow danced "The Cheshire Round,"
Till the pail was broken and the milk ran on the ground.
Over the hills and a great way off,
The wind shall blow my top-knot off.

He met old Dame Trot with a basket of eggs,
He used his pipe and she used her legs;
She danced about till the eggs were all broke,
She began for to fret, but he laughed at the joke.
Over the hills and a great way off,
The wind shall blow my top-knot off.

Tom saw a cross fellow was beating an ass,
Heavy laden with pots, pans, dishes, and glass;
He took out his pipe and he played them a tune,
And the poor donkey's load was lightened full soon.
  Over the hills and a great way off,
  The wind shall blow my top-knot off.

Kintu

by ELIZABETH ENRIGHT

illustrated by BOBRI

THE JUNGLE VILLAGE

Kintu was a little black boy who lived in Africa. He lived
with his father and mother and his five brothers and sisters
in a big mud hut with a straw roof, shaped like a beehive.
The beehive in which Kintu lived was the largest of a great
group of beehives in the middle of the jungle, for Kintu's
father, Kitomba, was the chief of his tribe, and therefore a
very important person. Kintu was his eldest son, which
meant that he, too, would one day be a chief.

He had two brothers and three sisters to play with.
There was Timbo, who could throw a spear farther than
Kintu could, although he was a year younger. And there
were Kakopa and Kaku, who were twins and who looked so
much alike that Kakopa had to wear a ring in her nose so
that people could tell which was which. Then there was
Wapi, who was fat, and rather bowlegged, and always eating something. And last of all there was Nomba, who was
the baby and who spent most of her time in a little ham-
mock which hung from her mother's shoulders.

They were very busy children; their days were filled with lessons—most exciting ones. Kintu had more of these than anyone else, because he was the eldest son and to be a chief you must know many things.

You must know, for instance, how to throw a spear faultlessly, how to shoot an arrow perfectly; and every day Kintu practiced for hours, hurling his spear and shooting his arrows at a red circle painted on the trunk of a baobab tree.

He learned how to play the drums, and with the palms of his hands make them talk the drum language which in Africa is the way that messages are sent from village to village.

"Look out, look out," say the drums, beating deeply, "an enemy tribe is coming down the river"; or "Look out, look out, an angry storm approaches from the east!" Usually they send warning messages but sometimes they only converse together.

Kintu would sit with his drum before him, his hands thumping on the tightly stretched skin, and for miles around the jungle murmured with the sounds he made.

A chief's son must be able to dance to the drums as well as to play them. Kintu learned devil dances, and fever dances, dances of triumph, dances to bring good hunting, or fine weather, or the rain, and all of them were different. Kintu liked the devil dances best because when he did them, he wore a magnificent headdress made of crimson feathers and telephone wire. (His father considered the telephone wire a great bargain; he had got it from a white trader who had passed that way several years before, and he had only given four leopard skins and a pair of elephant's tusks in exchange for a big coil of it. They used it for all sorts of things: Kintu's mother wove it into their head-dresses, and made baskets out of it; it even held their roof together in places.)

The devil dances took longer than any of the others, and were more interesting because there was a great deal of leaping and shouting to them. The drumbeats grew louder and louder till your ears rang with the sound of them, and you kept on dancing till you fell exhausted in the dust, and had to be taken home.

Kintu learned many other things, too. He was taught how to cure the hides of wild animals, and how to make arrowheads and spearheads of metal and stone. He learned how to kindle a fire with two sticks, how to set a trap, how to climb trees almost as fast as a monkey. He learned which berries were poisonous, and which ones were the best cure for snakebite.

Timbo and Wapi had lessons much the same as his own, but Kakopa and Kaku learned other things: they made pottery and cooked and wove mats of grass and palm leaves. They had their dances, too. All of the children were dressed alike in little colored skirts except for Nomba who was attired simply in a bracelet and a head necklace. All of them had brass ornaments on their ankles and around their necks, and would have felt strange without the quiet jingling which accompanied their walking.

Every day the children awoke at the very first light of dawn, and rising from the hard earth which was the only bed they had, shook themselves like little dogs and walked straight out of the hut to work or play as they pleased. Kintu took up his spear and practiced throwing it. Kakopa and Kaku wove their mats; and Timbo and Wapi played leapfrog or pretended to be hunters stalking a panther in the jungle. Nomba was too fat and too young to do anything but lie in the sun, chewing a piece of sugar cane.

In the middle of the morning, their mother made a fire by rubbing two sticks together till a spark caught the leaves and kindling on the flat stone which was her fireplace. Then in a great earthenware pot she cooked their breakfast—corn and manioc root and eggs (and sometimes chicken).

When it was done she called them, and they all sat down around the big pot and dipped into it with their fingers. Wapi usually managed to get the most, and often burned himself because he never could bear to wait for things to cool.

Their only other meal was in the evening and was usually exactly the same as the first; but sometimes as a special treat, their mother made them a delicious pudding of corn flour and palm oil and dried white caterpillars.

After supper the people of the village would gather around a fire and talk or sing. The men spoke of hunting, and the oldest ones had stories to tell of the times when lions were fiercer and elephants bigger than any found nowadays. Kintu, sitting beside his father, would shiver and try not to listen, because though nobody knew it, he was afraid of the jungle!

MAGIC

Now living in a jungle is very much like living next door to the zoo, except that the animals are not in cages, which makes quite a difference. Sometimes at night Kintu would lie awake and listen to the strange sounds made by wild creatures in the jungle, and be very afraid.

There was an insect which ticked all night long like a little watch, and an insect which made a loud noise like an alarm clock. There were the excited voices of suddenly awakened monkeys, and the croaking of big frogs which sounded like old men talking together in deep hoarse voices. There were panthers and leopards whose snarls were like the sound of thick canvas being torn. And there were the grunts of hippopotami who left the river and walked on land at night. There were noises made by nightjars and cicadas, and all the other hundreds of creatures who preferred to do their talking after dark.

Kintu would lie on his hard earthen bed and shake with fright, because he knew that when he was older his father would expect him to hunt in the jungle and to know it as well as he knew his own village. It would never do for a chief's son to be afraid!

It worried Kintu badly, and finally he decided to go and see the witch doctor and ask him for a spell to make him braver.

So one morning, after breakfast, he stole away from his brothers and sisters and playmates, and all by himself walked to the witch doctor's hut.

It was set apart from the rest of the village, and on either side of the door were little idols carved of black wood. One had a very ugly, cross face, and one grinned from ear to ear showing a double row of square, ivory teeth. Kintu bowed and raised his spear to each of them, then he entered the hut and came face to face with the witch doctor.

The witch doctor was very old and very wise, and he wore a derby hat, which he had got from the same trader who brought the telephone wire. From his great height he looked down at Kintu, without smiling; and Kintu would have shaken in his shoes if he had any to shake in.

"Chief's son," said the witch doctor, "why have you come to see me?"

"Witch doctor," began Kintu bravely, "I am in great trouble. I am afraid of the jungle!" He paused, and glanced up to see if the witch doctor looked disapproving, but there was no change in the old man's expression, so he continued. "Yes, I'm afraid of it. All of it. Its beasts, its noises and its huge trees. I don't even like the way it smells. How can I ever be a great chief like my father when I am such a coward?"

He hung his head for he was very much ashamed.

"This is bad!" said the witch doctor. "I must think." And he sat down on the floor, pulled his derby hat over his nose and thought. Kintu leaned against the wall and watched him almost without breathing, he was so terribly excited.

After several minutes (long ones, they seemed) the witch doctor stood up, pushing back his hat. Still without smiling he looked down at Kintu.

"Chief's son," he said, "I believe I have a cure for you."

He leaned down, took something out of a red earthenware

bowl, and put it into Kintu's little black hand.

"Take this," he said, "and tomorrow, when the sun is at its highest, walk three hundred paces into the jungle towards the east. After you have walked for three hundred paces, plant this charm at the foot of the first baobab tree you find; then, when you have buried it, say these words—" (But what the words were I cannot tell you for they were black magic, and a secret.)

"In the jungle? All by myself?" asked Kintu in a timid voice.

"All by yourself, chief's son," said the witch doctor firmly.

Kintu walked slowly home. Once he stopped and opened his hand to see what the charm was like; it was nothing but the dry stone of a fruit and didn't look as though it had much magic in it; but the witch doctor had said it had, and Kintu believed him.

That evening he couldn't eat his supper and his mother was worried about him.

"You have been eating between meals again," she said. "When *will* you learn to leave that monkey-bread tree alone?"

But Kintu only sighed, and said nothing. Very late that night he lay awake and listened to the jungle sounds which seemed louder and more terrifying than ever. He thought the cicadas were chanting a jeering song: "Afraid, afraid, afraid," they cried, over and over again.

"Perhaps after tomorrow you'll be singing another song," whispered Kintu into the darkness; and feeling a little more cheerful, he went to sleep.

52

The next day dawned bright and very hot; and Kintu went through his duties in a daze.

When, soon after their morning meal, the sun had ridden to its highest point, and everybody else had gone to sleep in the shade, Kintu picked up his spear, and holding the charm in his other hand, tiptoed through the drowsy village and into the jungle.

It was hot and steamy under the great trees; it smelled like the inside of a greenhouse, warm and damp. Everywhere the silk cotton trees raised their great trunks; and high, high overhead a whole, separate airy world existed: parrots called in cross voices, a thousand birds sang different songs, and monkeys leapt nimbly along the boughs, chattering and scolding.

Counting all the time, and forgetting to be afraid, Kintu looked up and stubbed his toe badly on a root. By this time he had walked his first hundred paces and was beginning his second hundred. The farther he walked the wilder the jungle grew, and he had to beat back the undergrowth and tear apart the vines which hung, covered with flowers, from every tree.

Once he surprised a group of little brown monkeys who were sitting sociably on the ground in a circle, eating berries. They simply leapt up the trunk of a palm tree when they saw him, and sat high in the leaves telling him what they thought of him till long after he had passed.

Great moths flew blindly into his face; and once he came upon a hibiscus bush so beautiful, with its flaming red flowers, that he stopped and stared at it.

All this time he had forgotten about being afraid, but now as he came to the middle of his last hundred paces the shadows seemed suddenly darker, and the trees taller than before, and he found himself counting more and more rapidly.

"Two hundred and eighty," said Kintu, leaping over a log, "two hundred and eighty-one—eighty-two—eighty-three . . ." On his right something gave a squeal and plunged into the bushes.

"Eighty-four, eighty-five," shouted Kintu in a loud, bold voice (he was running now), "eighty-six, eighty-seven, eighty-eight, eighty-nine . . ."

At last the three hundred paces were behind him, and he began to look about for a baobab tree.

There were silk cotton trees, and gum trees, and pandanus trees, and borassus trees, and ebony trees, and rubber trees, and mahogany trees, and kakula trees; but there was not a single baobab tree in sight!

Kintu sighed; his heart was beating like a tom-tom and the palms of his hands felt cold and damp; but he had come this far and he simply couldn't turn back till he had buried the magic fruit pit.

So he hunted and he hunted, and went farther and farther into the jungle, and at last he came upon an enormous baobab tree standing all by itself in a clearing.

He felt safer somehow now that he had found it, and with relief he knelt among its great roots and scooped out a hole in the ground with the head of his spear; he buried the charm and covered it with earth. After that, he said the

words of black magic which the witch doctor had taught him.

Then he picked up his spear and started back.

It had taken him a long time to find the baobab tree and by now it was the middle of the afternoon; the shadows were growing longer.

A crowd of little gnats circled around his head as he walked, buzzing in high thin voices till his ears rang and he felt dizzy. He kept waving his spear at them to drive them away, but they didn't mind it in the least and came back again as soon as he stopped.

On and on stumbled Kintu, among flowers, and tendrils, and great leaves. He realized that he had lost his way, and that so far the magic had not worked, because he felt more frightened than ever.

He thought about his family all safe together in the village, and wondered when they would miss him and begin to look for him. He thought about the stories, told by the old hunters, of fierce lions who sometimes come into the jungle at night, of hyenas whose cry is like the laughter of a devil-god, of great elephants with tusks of ivory who can uproot small trees with their trunks. He thought about the buried fruit pit and the magic words, and they seemed small protection against the jungle and its many dangers. He wished that he had never gone to see the witch doctor at all, and that he had allowed himself to be a coward in peace.

Kintu began to cry quietly, because he was sure that he would never see his family again, and he was terribly afraid. He stopped walking and stood very still among great ferns like giant feather dusters. It seemed foolish to go on when whatever direction he took was bound to be the wrong one.

It was growing darker now, and already the tree toads had begun their evening conversation. "Wack-a-wack-a-wack," they cried in harsh voices from every tree. The gnats, fortunately, had got tired of Kintu's waving spear and had all gone off together to find some other creature to torment; so except for the remarks of the tree toads, and the occasional cry of a bird, it seemed very still.

Then, all at once, quite near, he heard a sound like that of thick canvas being torn in two. The snarl of a leopard!

It no longer seemed useless to go on; in fact, it seemed most necessary to go somewhere very quickly; and Kintu, spear in hand, began to run faster than he had ever run before.

Ahead of him, six little monkeys, who had also heard the dangerous sound, went leaping and skipping along the ground at great speed. Kintu, feeling somehow that they were his friends, followed them; and when they came to a huge tree hung with creepers which the monkeys swarmed neatly up, like little sailors climbing up a rigging, he went right after them as fast as he could go.

Up and up he struggled, with his spear between his strong teeth, and his little black fingers and toes curling around the thick vine almost as cleverly as the monkeys' did. The creeper looped itself over one of the lower branches and returned to earth on the other side, so Kintu began climbing up the boughs: Stretch, pull, swing! Stretch, pull, swing!—till he had nearly reached the top of the tree; and then he sat down on a huge limb with his

shoulder against the broad trunk, and his spear across his
knees. His heart was thumping like anything and he was
out of breath, but he felt slightly safer.

The six little monkeys, who didn't seem to mind him at all, sat on a branch just above him, and said things very fast in monkey language about leopards. Kintu wished that he could understand them and join in their conversation; he wanted to ask them if leopards were any good at climbing trees. Still, even if he couldn't speak to them, it was a comfort just to have them there, and he hoped they wouldn't go away.

All about him stretched the strange leaves and branches of jungle trees, and below him he saw the great ferns and flowers through which he had beaten his way. Overhead the sky was a darker blue, with a little purple in it, and already there was a star, pale and cold, shining just over the place where the sun had set.

The air was filled with queer smells. A clump of yellow orchids bloomed in a deserted bird's nest several feet below him, and gave off a perfume so strong and heavy that he grew tired of it very soon. There were big red berries on a tree nearby that had an odor rather like cough medicine; and you've been in the monkey house at the zoo, haven't you? So you know how the monkeys smelled.

It was really twilight, now; and Kintu saw the bright busy lights of fireflies everywhere. Huge mosquitoes came whining out of the shadows; cicadas sang at the tops of their voices; and the tree toads almost screamed at each other. An evening wind stirred for a moment in the feathery treetops and moved the branch above Kintu where the monkeys were dozing in a row. It woke them up, and they chattered anxiously at each other for a minute. But they soon went back to sleep; and Kintu, feeling like the loneliest person on earth, continued to stare at the sparkling patterns made by fireflies against the darkness.

Presently the moon rose, huge and lopsided, above the

world; each leaf glittered in its light, and the brass bracelets on Kintu's ankle looked as if they were made of purest gold.

The night was full of sounds: rustling sounds and scratchings and scamperings, squeaks and grunts in the darkness below, the singing of the night birds in the leaves above.

Then Kintu heard another sound—a new one. He heard the heavy, soft footsteps of an enormous creature stepping quietly, the snapping of shrubs and the squelching sound of wet earth under huge feet. He leaned forward and peered still more intently into the blackness below him. A tremendous shape, darker than the shadows from which it came, moved gently and ponderously towards the tree where he was hidden. Bigger than a house, it looked; almost as big as a mountain, Kintu thought. Slowly, slowly the Thing approached; then paused directly below him. Suddenly there was a faint sound of scraping, and the tree began to quiver as though in an earthquake; the monkeys jabbered nervously; and Kintu knew that an elephant, the largest of all wild creatures, was scratching his back on a branch.

Then slowly, as before, the great beast went on its way; the noise of snapping twigs and heavy tread grew fainter, and it was seen no more.

Hours passed; the moon was high in the sky; and Kintu, too tired to think of fear any longer, settled himself against the tree trunk and slept with the monkeys.

THE LEOPARD

He must have slept a long time, because when the shrill, excited voices of the monkeys woke him, he saw that the moon had set, and the world was as black as the inside of a pocket.

He looked down wondering what was the matter. At first he saw nothing but the roaming lights of the fireflies. And then a chill of fear ran up the calves of his legs and along his spine to the nape of his neck; for below him he saw two small lights, side by side, which did not move; two small lights which he knew were the eyes of an animal watching him.

Squealing and scolding, the monkeys bounded along the branches, dived into the boughs of another tree and were gone.

Kintu faced real danger, alone.

Once more he heard the low snarl which had so frightened him earlier in the evening. The leopard had found him, after all.

The two lights moved a little; Kintu knew that the animal was crouching, making sure of the distance before he sprang.

Then the eyes leapt forward; there was the swish of a

heavy body flying through the air, the impact of it against the tree, and the sound of sharp claws tearing wood.

Determinedly, the leopard climbed the tree towards Kintu.

It was useless to be frightened now. Something would have to be done, and quickly too.

Swiftly and quietly Kintu stood up on the branch. He held on to the trunk with his left hand, and in his right he

raised the spear high above his shoulder.

He could hardly see the dark shape of the animal climbing towards him, but he would have to take a chance.

"Now or never," said Kintu in a small voice, and hurled the spear.

Then there was a grunt and the thud of a soft, heavy weight falling upon the earth. After that there were no more sounds at all: and Kintu knew that the leopard would not bother him again. Not this one, anyway.

Trembling all over, but almost shouting with triumph, he climbed, feeling his way, a little higher in the tree. How glad he was, now, that his father had made him practice throwing the spear hour after hour, day after day.

"I certainly won't sleep again," said Kintu; and slept.

DRUMBEATS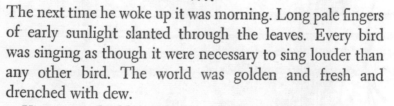

The next time he woke up it was morning. Long pale fingers of early sunlight slanted through the leaves. Every bird was singing as though it were necessary to sing louder than any other bird. The world was golden and fresh and drenched with dew.

Kintu stretched his stiff arms and legs, and yawned with a great noise. He looked for his spear and wondered for a moment if he had dropped it. Then he remembered about the leopard.

Quickly he climbed down the branches and slid along the creepers to the ground.

There, stretched at the foot of the tree, lay the leopard, so beautiful with its tawny dark-spotted fur that Kintu was sorry he had killed it. But when he looked closer and saw the cruel curving white teeth, and the glittering claws half hidden in the soft paws, he was sorry no longer.

"It is better to kill than to be killed," said Kintu wisely; and pulling his spear from the leopard's hide, he started off once more to find his village.

It was a beautiful morning! Wet leaves glittered in the sun like leaves of gold. Great drops of dew fell on his head; and there was a little pool in the cup of every flower.

Feeling thirsty, he tipped a big leaf down to his open

mouth, and water poured into it as if from a pitcher.

He was hungry, too, and stopped for a minute to pull some purple berries from a vine. Nothing had ever tasted so delicious.

He felt like a king as he strode through the jungle, brandishing his spear and singing: "I am not afraid!"

The wild creatures, watching him, knew that this was true.

"He is not afraid," screamed the gray parrots in the treetops. "He is not afraid," sang all the birds together. "He is not afraid, he is not afraid," chattered the noisy monkeys; and great serpents, sunning themselves on branches, watched him through the leaves, and said in slow voices, "He is not afraid."

The leopards saw him, too, and the black panther with golden eyes, hidden behind a screen of flowers. "No, he is not afraid," they said, and turned away into the shadows feeling fear themselves.

Never had Kintu been so happy; he was filled with hope, and was sure that he would find his village, and that everything would be all right after all. He listened with joy to all the shrieking, babbling, singing, chattering noises of the early morning jungle. He liked its noises. He loved the way it smelled.

Then something made him stop, quite still, in his tracks. He held his breath, and listened with ears which had been trained to sharpness by the jungle, to another sound. Far, far to the right of him, there was a faint throbbing in the air. Yes! There could be no doubt about it; it was the beating of drums that he heard and this is what they were saying:

"Chief Kitomba's eldest son has disappeared. Has he been seen? Has he been seen?"

And then, still farther away, to his left, the drums of another village replied, "Chief Kitomba's son has not been seen. Chief Kitomba's son has not been seen."

Kintu's heart skipped a beat. The drums which had spoken first were the drums of his village, he knew. If he turned to the right and followed their sound he would surely find his way home.

He couldn't go fast enough! He ran; and skipped over creepers and leapt high in the air, twirling his spear, and yelling for joy. But he did not forget to stop now and then and make a scratch on the bark of a tree with his spearhead. When he got back to the village he would ask some of the men to get the leopard for him. And he wanted them to be

sure and find it.

The jungle was loud with the sound of drumbeats now. All the villages for miles around were answering the message from his village, and relaying it to others still farther away.

It grew very hot; yellow mist rose from the damp ground. The gnats came after him in swarms; but he didn't care: the world was beautiful and exciting and full of adventures, and he was no longer afraid.

Then he saw the hibiscus bush with its scarlet flowers, the very same one that he had noticed the day before; and he knew that he was near his home! He broke one of the bright blossoms from its stem and stuck it behind his ear as a badge of triumph.

There was a shout behind him suddenly, and turning he saw his father running towards him between the trees.

"Father!" cried Kintu, throwing his spear to the ground and leaping into Chief Kitomba's arms.

"I was lost! I spent the night in a tree, I saw an elephant, I killed a wicked leopard, and I'm not afraid," said Kintu all in one breath.

"You are safe, my son; you are not hurt?" asked Chief Kitomba anxiously.

"No, but I am very, *very* hungry," answered Kintu.

THE CELEBRATION

His mother was so glad to see him that she cooked him the special pudding which is made of corn flour and palm oil

68

and dried white caterpillars. Then she stood over him and watched to see that he ate it all.

His brothers and sisters sat round him in a circle, each of their mouths hanging open an inch, and listened to the story of his night in the jungle. He had to tell it three times.

"Let us play a game about it," said Wapi to Timbo. "You can be the leopard and I will be Kintu in the tree."

"No, indeed," said Timbo. "You forget that I'm the eldest. *I* will be Kintu, and *you* can be the leopard!"

All the people of the village were so glad that Kintu returned and was unharmed, that Chief Kitomba said, "Light the bonfires; bring out the big drums; we will have a jubilee, as soon as the leopard's brought back to the village."

"A jubilee!" screamed everybody in delight, and clapped their hands and ran to fetch wood for the bonfires. Half a dozen men followed Kintu's markings to the place where the slain leopard lay beneath a tall tree. Cutting a slim strong sapling with their knives they lashed the heavy animal to it and, raising the burden to their strong right shoulders, walked singing and laughing back to the village. When they had reached it they went at once to the hut of Kintu's father, and set the leopard down beside the door. Everybody came to look at it, and said what a big one it was, and what a fine coat it had, and how wicked and dangerous it must have been when it was alive.

Kintu could feel happiness and pride swelling inside of his chest like a big balloon. His ribs felt almost too narrow to hold it. He looked downwards and drew a circle in the dust with his big toe.

"Now we will celebrate," said Chief Kitomba.

Kintu went into the hut and put on his favorite headdress of crimson feathers and telephone wire, for he felt that this was a very special occasion. Then he walked to the central clearing in the village where all the tribe was gathered.

The fires had been lighted, and were burning like five great towers of flame and smoke, soaring and snapping. Half a dozen of the bravest warriors in the village stood behind the big drums, waiting to play them.

"Come here, my son," said Chief Kitomba, and Kintu went to him. Around his neck his father fastened a necklace made of leopards' teeth; and around his waist he tied a leopard's skin so that the tail hung down behind just as

it should.

"Now dance," said Chief Kitomba, and Kintu for the first time in his life was allowed to do the Dance of the Victorious Hunter; for had he not killed the leopard, that creature feared and hated by all jungle dwellers, men and beasts alike?

"Boom. Boom. Boom-a-diddy-boom!" sang the drums, and Kintu's feet moved swiftly through the dust, hopping and leaping. Around him all the people of the village clapped their hands and stamped in time to the music.

Kintu finished his dance with a whoop and a yell. And then everybody danced!

Drums boomed, brass anklets jingled, spears clashed together, dry gourds were shaken like rattles, people sang, and

monkeys screamed in the thickets. Never had there been such a loud and joyful jubilee in the history of the village!

It went on till very late at night. They brought out delicious things to eat: hot things in big earthenware pots, fruits of all kinds on round platters. There were delicious things to drink, too, in tall black jars.

Long after it was dark the fires still burned high, and the village was filled with flickering lights and dark moving shadows.

Everyone was happy, and Kintu was the happiest of all, for his father had said to him, "I am well pleased with you, my son; you will be a good chief to our people when I am gone. Only fear can make a strong man weak, and you have conquered that."

At last, when they had all grown tired of dancing and

73

had eaten too much, they sat down around one of the dying bonfires and asked Kintu to tell them his story.

He told them about climbing the tree after the monkeys and about the elephant who had come unsuspectingly so near to him; he told them all about the leopard. But he did not tell them why he had gone into the jungle in the first place or about the magic charm; that was a secret between the witch doctor and himself and the baobab tree.

Finally, when he was sure that he couldn't stay awake more than two minutes longer, Kintu stood up and said goodnight to all his proud, well-fed relatives and friends. But before he went to his father's hut, he tiptoed through the shadowy village to the hut which was surrounded by little black idols. The witch doctor was leaning in his doorway.

"Well, chief's son," he said, and from his great height he looked down at Kintu without smiling. But this time Kintu was not timid in the least.

"Well, witch doctor," he said, "I am very grateful to you. I did everything you told me to, and then I got lost. I spent the night in the jungle among wild creatures; I even killed a leopard. And this morning when I woke up, I knew I wasn't frightened any more!"

The witch doctor didn't look very much impressed.

Kintu waited for him to speak. At last he nodded his head slowly up and down and said "Good." That was all, but Kintu felt that it was enough.

Turning, he left the witch doctor's hut and walked slowly through the darkness. It was quieter, now. There were occasional bursts of laughter from groups of people,

but the voices were subdued, and the fires had died into heaps of glowing coals.

Kintu entered his hut and removed the headdress of crimson feathers and telephone wire. Then he lay down on the earth against the wall. Above the voices and the laughter he heard the night sounds of the jungle. He heard the tree toads, and the monkeys, and the insects which tick like little watches. Far, far away he heard a sound like that of thick canvas being torn in two. Kintu knew that another leopard roamed the jungle, terrifying all creatures. He reached out and patted the handle of his spear companionably.

But above all these noises he was aware of the song of the cicadas. No longer could he make the words "Afraid, afraid, afraid" fit their chanting. There were no words for it. The thousands of voices pulsed together like the sound of a heart beating, and the longer Kintu listened to them the drowsier he became. And at last with his cheek pressed against the earth and with one hand on his spear he went to sleep.

Mike Fink

an American Tall Tale

by MICHAEL GORHAM

illustrated by RICHARD BENNETT

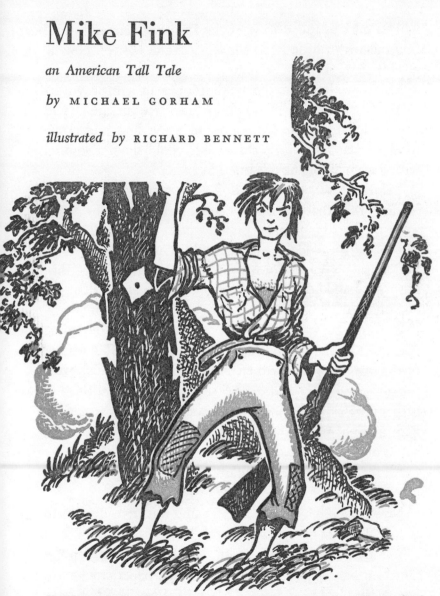

Text from *The Real Book of American Tall Tales*, copyright, 1952, by Franklin Watts, Inc., and published by Garden City Books.

Mike Fink was called King of the Keelboatmen, and you'll find out why a little later. First, I want to tell you how he got his start.

Mike was born on the wild frontier in a little village called Pittsburgh. He could chop down trees before he had his second teeth. He knew how to use a bow and arrow when he was just a little shaver. He could shoot a squirrel with it even before he'd learned to cuss.

Before he was dry behind the ears, he had a muzzle-loading rifle that he called "Bang-All." One day when some men held a shooting match, young Mike tried to join in. At first they kidded him and told him to go back home and finish his chores for his mother. Mike didn't like this. He argued and he bragged. "I shoot big when old Bang-All and my shoulder get together. I can outshoot any of you."

The men guffawed. This shooting match was a big thing, because a farmer had put up a cow for a prize. The winner of the match would get the cow's hide and fat, which were the most valuable parts. The second, third, fourth, and fifth prizes were the meat. And the man who came sixth had the right to dig the lead bullets out of the targets. He could melt them down and make new bullets.

All the men had paid a quarter for each shot they would take at the target.

Now Mike plunked down $1.25 and took five chances to shoot. "I aim to get the whole cow," he boasted.

The men jeered at him again, and began setting up the targets which were little pieces of white paper stuck onto boards that had been burned black in a fire. The bull's-eye was a small hole in the middle of the white paper where the blackened board showed through. It took a good shot to hit the paper at sixty yards, and a real expert to hit the bull's-eye. Most of the men in the shooting match *were* experts. They could drive a nail into a board by firing at its head. Many of them hit the bull's-eye. There wasn't a one who couldn't "eat paper"—which meant hitting the paper around the bull's-eye.

Mike shot last, because he was the last one to pay his money. He raised Bang-All, took aim, and fired. The men roared. "You didn't even eat paper!"

Mike shouted back, "Talk loud when you've something to say. I hit the bull's-eye." And the men found out that sure enough he had. But that wasn't all. Mike had hit the exact center of the bull's-eye, and he'd won the cow's hide and fat, because his shot was better than any of the others.

"Just luck," the men grumbled.

Mike fired Bang-All again, and again he hit the exact center of the bull's-eye. Now he had won a quarter of the cow's meat.

"Anybody want to bet I'll get another quarter of beef?" Mike called out as he rammed powder and a bullet down Bang-All's barrel.

"I'll bet my powder horn you can't do it again, sonny," somebody yelled.

On the next shot, Mike won the beef *and* the powder horn.

Before he was through, Mike had won the whole cow, another powder horn, and a supply of bullets. As he started off leading the cow home, he grinned. "I saved you some trouble," he called back. "Now none of you have to carry a quarter of beef home. I always take five shots. That way I make the critter carry its own meat for me. . . . And next time call me *Mister* Fink."

It wasn't long before young Mike was ruled out of all shooting matches, because no one else had a chance. Farmers who put cows up for prizes announced that the hide and fat went to Mike Fink, who would *not* be allowed to shoot. That was the only way anybody else could get any beef.

But Mike began to get bored. He'd gone about as far as he could go in the shooting line around Pittsburgh. So he thought about what to do next.

The biggest and strongest men, Mike noticed, worked on the keelboats that went up and down the Ohio and Mississippi rivers between Pittsburgh and New Orleans. Every keelboatman had wonderful stories to tell of dangers on the river and fights with Indians or with pirates. The river was chock-full of adventure, and that's what Mike needed to keep him from dying of dry rot.

He went to the patroon—that was the captain—of a keelboat that was tied up at the dock. "I've come to work on your boat," he said.

"I only take men," the patroon said, "men that can shoot and fight and push a pole. Poling a keelboat up this river is a job for those who are half-horse and half-alligator. You're just a colt."

Mike didn't say a word. He just picked up a tin cup from the patroon's table, dipped it full of river water and balanced it on the head of a keelboatman who was leaning against a barrel fast asleep. Then he walked to the end of the boat, lifted Bang-All to his shoulder and fired. The cup

didn't budge. But, out of two neat holes drilled by Mike's bullet, cold river water spurted down over the keelboatman's head and woke him up.

He was riled plenty. "I ain't had a bath in six months," he roared, "and I aim to spifflicate whoever tried to give me one now."

"There might be some question about who'll do the spifflicating," Mike roared back. "I'm a regular screamer. Whoop! I can outrun, outshoot, outbrag, and outfight any man in this neck of the woods. Whoop! Come on and see how tough I am. I can strike a blow like a falling tree, and every lick I make in the woods lets in an acre of sunshine. I walk tall into a fight. I haven't had a tussle for two whole livelong days and my muscles are as rusty as an old hinge. Cockadoodle-doo!"

Mike flapped his arms like a rooster's wings.

"Come ashore where we got plenty of room," the keelboatman shouted.

On shore they faced each other in the middle of the muddy street. Mike took off his buckskin jacket and the keelboatman shed his red shirt. They grabbed each other by the neck and started to heave and pull.

"Do we fight fair," Mike asked between grunts, "or is this rough and tumble?"

"Rough and tumble," the keelboatman grunted back.

"That's the way I like it," Mike hollered. "That makes a fight more interesting." And he bit the keelboatman's left ear. Then he stomped on his feet, punched him in the stomach, grabbed his hair with both hands, and slammed the keelboatman's face down on his knee.

The keelboatman fought back, scratching with his fingers and flailing out with his powerful arms. They gave each other bear hugs and shoved back and forth all over the street, until finally Mike saw his chance. With one powerful hand Mike grabbed the keelboatman's neck, with the other he took hold of his pants and, giving a mighty heave, he swung the man up in the air, then staggered to the river's edge and threw him in.

"You can fight all right, manny," the patroon said. "But can you work?"

Mike showed that he could work, and he made his first trip to New Orleans. Now he was a keelboatman, with a red shirt of his own, brown overalls called "butternut britches," a blue jacket and a leather cap. Of all the tough men on the frontier, the keelboatmen were the toughest,

and it wasn't long before Mike showed he was the toughest of keelboatmen. He learned the songs of the river and bellowed them out in his deep voice. He saved the patroon the expense of buying a horn, which every keelboat needed to warn other boats it was coming. Mike could make sounds more like a horn than the horn itself could.

At night when the boat tied up, Mike danced on shore, and in the daytime he often danced on the flat top of the boat as it floated down the river. He kept a sharp eye out for Indians and river pirates when the boat nosed in close to shore. He learned how to use the boat's sail. And coming back up the river from New Orleans he learned a great deal

more.

Now the real work began—work for giants—work for men who were half-alligator and half-horse. For four long months, Mike and the other keelboatmen fought against the river's current to get the boat back up to Pittsburgh. Sometimes they rowed the boat with oars. Sometimes they used long poles to push the heavy craft upstream. Sometimes they "bushwhacked"—that is, they grabbed overhanging bushes and limbs of trees when they were close to shore and pulled the boat along. Or they walked on the bank and pulled the boat with a rope.

Mike rowed and poled and heaved with the best of them; and at night he could always have a good relaxing fight with his friends or with some stranger he met on shore. Before long he was head pole man, then steersman. He could steer a boat over the trickiest water, through rapids, and around hidden snags and sand bars. And then he got to be a patroon and could wear a red feather in his cap.

Mike wasn't satisfied with just one red feather. Every time he met another keelboat, he challenged its patroon to a fight. He always won and he always took that patroon's feather and put it in his own cap. Soon he looked like an Indian chief. About that time people began to call him "King of the Keelboatmen."

Now along about the middle of one trip down the river, Mike ran out of food. His keelboat was carrying a cargo of snuff, and the men could only eat just so much of that. Then Mike saw a fine flock of sheep in a clearing on the shore, and he thought to himself that some mutton would be a mighty fine change of diet.

It would be easy enough to steal some sheep, but Mike never liked to do things the easy way. That wouldn't be interesting enough. So he ordered the boat in to shore, knocked open a keg of snuff, took two great handfuls of it, and walked up among the sheep. Then he rubbed the snuff into several of the woolly faces.

While the sheep sneezed and coughed and pranced around, Mike sent a man to get the farmer who owned them. The farmer was amazed to see his animals, brown-faced, snorting, and rubbing their noses in the grass.

"I thought I ought to tell you that five of your sheep are sick," Mike said piously. "I saw a lot of this same sickness up the river. The black murrain, it's called, and it's mighty catching. You'd better shoot those five sheep now, or you might lose the whole flock."

The farmer was frightened. He'd do anything to save his flock; but he said, "I dassent shoot the sick ones. I might hit some well ones instead. There's no man alive good enough to do that job, unless maybe it's Mike Fink."

Mike said modestly, "*My* name is Mike Fink."

Well, the upshot was that the farmer paid Mike one well sheep to shoot the five he thought were sick. Mike tossed the sheep into the river, and told the farmer he hoped nothing bad would happen to the rest of the flock.

Of course, after his boat had floated down the river and caught up with the sheep, Mike fished them out, and the keelboatmen had a wonderful feast that night.

Mike was always thinking of things to make life more exciting. One time he saw the patroon of another keelboat lying sound asleep. As Mike's boat floated up close, Mike

reached over with an oar and whacked the patroon on the head. That started a good fight, which was all Mike wanted.

But tricks like these began to add up, and finally Mike was in trouble with the law. There was a reward out in Louisville, Kentucky, for his arrest. Naturally, Mike didn't want to go to jail, but it happened that the constable in Louisville was a friend of his, and it seemed a pity to waste the reward. So Mike made an agreement with the constable that he would let himself be taken to court. Of course, Mike made the constable guarantee that he wouldn't actually be put in jail. And one more thing, too. Mike explained he didn't feel comfortable anywhere except on his boat. He'd go to court if he could go in his boat.

So a date was set. The constable arrested Mike, and Mike went to court in his boat. This is how he did it: He put wagon wheels under it and got a team of oxen to pull it up the hill.

When the judge called the case, the constable got his reward. Then he explained that he just couldn't find any witnesses against Mike. And the judge had to let Mike go free. But there were plenty of people in the courtroom who didn't appreciate Mike's sense of humor, and they hollered at the judge to put him in jail anyhow.

Just about then, Mike shouted to the other red-shirted keelboatmen, "Stand to your poles, mannies, and set off!"

Out through a window went Mike and his men. They climbed aboard their boat, cut loose the oxen, and gave a mighty heave with their poles. The boat on wheels rolled down the hill straight into the river, and Mike waved goodbye to Louisville.

Up to now, nothing on the frontier had ever got the best of Mike Fink. Then one Sunday morning he lost a fight— a fight with a bull. Mike's boat was pulled up by the shore, and he'd gone a little way along a clear creek to have a bath. He'd just taken his clothes off and was splashing himself in the water when he looked up and saw a huge bull.

For once, Mike wasn't eager to fight. He stepped aside as the bull charged at him. The bull landed in the water, and came out madder than ever. It didn't help any that Mike picked up his red shirt and started to climb into it. The bull hooked the shirt this time as he sailed past. The next time the animal charged, Mike decided he'd better get where its horns couldn't reach him. So he grabbed the bull's tail and hung on.

There he was, flapping out behind like clothes on a line in a high wind. The bull tore around all over the pasture till Mike was pretty well tuckered out. So, when he saw the limb of a tree overhead, Mike grabbed it and swung up to safety. For a while, everything was all right, but suddenly Mike jostled into a hornet's nest on the next limb up. About then he gave one big jump—and landed on the bull's back.

The bull lit out like a cyclone from the southwest. Right up to the pasture fence he went and then stopped dead in his tracks. Mike didn't stop, though. He sailed on over and landed smack in a churchyard, just as folks were coming out of church.

Mike always claimed that he would have gone back and fought that bull to a standstill if it hadn't been Sunday morning. As it was, he felt kind of conspicuous there at the church without his Sunday clothes on. So he streaked it toward his boat on the river before any of the churchgoers had had a chance to give a second gasp.

Now you may think from all this fighting and boat work of Mike's that he'd lost interest in Bang-All, his rifle. But that's not so. Mike always had Bang-All with him on his keelboat. He kept in practice by shooting holes in tin cups balanced on the keelboatmen's heads.

It was lucky he did keep in practice, because one time he accidentally bumped into a nest of pirates at a place called Cave-in-Rock. Mike knew he was in pirate country, but

there was such a storm on the river that he had to tie up
at the shore. The pirates knew he was coming down the
river, because they always had scouts out, watching for keelboats with valuable cargoes.

Well, the long and short of it was that Mike and Bang-
All cleaned out the whole batch of pirates, and they didn't

get going there at Cave-in-Rock again until about the time a young boatman named Abe Lincoln started taking cargoes down the river.

Mike had been half-alligator, half-horse on the Mississippi and Ohio rivers for a long time when he began to notice that things were changing. Houses along the shore were so close together now they were only a few miles apart. The river didn't seem to Mike much like the frontier any more. He got to feeling nervous and lonesome with so much civilization around. And then something happened that was more than he could stand. A boat that was run by a steam engine started to carry cargoes up and down the river. It didn't need men who were half-alligator, half-horse. Every time Mike saw this steamboat he got madder and madder. The steamboat would blow its whistle as much as to say, "Keelboats, get out of the way!"

Now Mike wasn't in the habit of getting out of anybody's way. One day the steamboat came puffing up the river as Mike's keelboat was floating down. Unless Mike or the steamboat changed course, there would be a collision.

The steersman asked Mike what to do.

"I'll steer," Mike shouted and took the tiller. "I'm a ring-tailed squealer," he roared. "I'm a regular screamer from the old Mississipp'. Whoop! I'm half wild horse and half cockeyed alligator, and the rest of me is crooked snags and red-hot snappin' turtle. Come on, you steamboat, and see how tough I am to chaw. I'm just spoiling for exercise. Cockadoodle-doo!"

The steersman saw the big steamboat looming up over the little keelboat, and he still wanted to know what Mike was going to do.

"Sink her!" Mike roared, looking dark and angry at the

steamboat.

By this time, the pilot on the steamboat had noticed Mike, and he let loose blast after warning blast from his whistle. And Mike answered with his boathorn voice, to let the big steamboat know that *it* had better get out of the way.

Then came the sudden terrific bump and the crash of breaking timbers. Half the members of Mike's crew were thrown into the river, and his keelboat sank in a minute, because her cargo was heavy. It was all bars of lead to be made into bullets. As she went down, Mike yelled to the crew to swim ashore. When he climbed up out of the water, he shook himself and squatted down, looking disgustedly at the river. He had lost a fight. And he didn't even get much satisfaction from watching the steamboat struggling upstream with a big hole in its side.

Pretty soon Mike stood up and announced, "I'm leaving the river. I always said I would if I lost a fight. Now I'm going out west where the frontier is and where things aren't so crowded and a man hasn't any of these smoking, clattering contraptions to worry about. It's time for Bang-All and me to get on the move."

Mike Fink went on to Missouri, where he joined the great fur traders of the West. He and Bang-All made great names for themselves there, just as they had on the river and in Pittsburgh when that little town had been on the frontier. To his dying day, Mike could still outrun, outjump, outshoot, outfight any man on both sides of the river from Pittsburgh to New Orleans, back again to St. Louis and all the way west. Whoop! Cockadoodle-doo!

Kiki Goes to Camp

written and illustrated

by CHARLOTTE STEINER

Kiki was going to camp. She could hardly wait.
She had been looking at camp pictures all winter long.
And *her* camp was going to be the most fun,
because there was a barn and a horse called Brownie.
Kiki loved horses!

Kiki had a hard time getting ready.
Every day she changed her mind about what toys
to take in her trunk.
Finally Mother said the trunk was filled with shorts
and sweaters, slacks and swimming suits, and all her
other camp clothes. She would have to carry whatever
toy she wanted. So Kiki took Coco, her toy horse.
She loved him more even than her dolls or Teddy Bear.
Kiki was sure Coco would like camp too.

When it was time to start, Kiki didn't want to leave her Mommy. But she felt better when the train started. She and Coco looked out the window and they even saw some horses.

It was dark before they arrived at Camp Rainbow, but the next morning it was exciting to wake up when the bugle called

Good Morning
A new day is dawning
Sun is up, sun is up, sun is up.

Kiki was a Sunbeam.
She and the other Sunbeams in her cabin had to hurry to get dressed. But they had time to peek out the window

AND—

there was a little rabbit looking at them.

At breakfast
they told the counselor
about the rabbit they saw.

It was fun to hurry back and help get the cabin
ready for morning inspection. Kiki swept the cabin
and the other campers made their
own beds. It was like playing house.

Kiki hoped she could take Coco down to
the barnyard to visit Brownie, the horse.
But swimming came next. And that was wonderful.
Kiki could hardly wait for swimming every day.
Kiki learned to hold her breath under water.

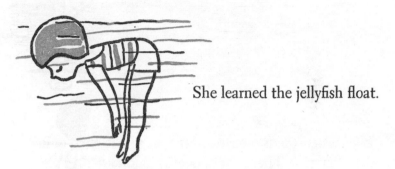

She learned the jellyfish float.

She learned how to kick.

And finally she could dog-paddle.

Then she was allowed to go in the rowboat with the
counselor and learn how to row.

Somehow there never was time to go see Brownie.
Even when the Sunbeams went on a hike they didn't
pass the barn. They sang songs while they walked
and picked berries whenever they saw some.

They collected leaves and stones
and animals for the nature exhibit.

They saw a lizard and they saw a butterfly.

And Kiki caught a frog.
Kiki had to take good care of the frog in the nature exhibit.

She loved the bigger animals too. The baby lambs
and the mother lamb were so soft.

And when the counselor found a motherless fawn
the Sunbeams took charge of it. They all loved it
so much they took turns feeding it.

Kiki wanted to go see Brownie, but the next day it rained.
Some of the campers built houses for their little pets,
but Kiki drew horses.

The next morning the counselor said there was a surprise
down at the barn.
Kiki could hardly believe it.
THERE
was Brownie, the horse,
and best of all there was her brand-new colt.
Kiki had been saving a lump of sugar for Brownie
but now she tried to feed it to the colt.
Every time Kiki had a free period she hurried down
to the barnyard to visit Brownie and the colt. She
listened to Brownie whinny for her colt. Sometimes
Brownie whinnied at Kiki, too. Kiki loved Brownie
and the colt. The colt loved Kiki, too, and even
came looking for her when she was in her cabin.

Every day camp was more fun until time for Stunt
Night came. Kiki just didn't know what to do. Then
one day while she was talking to Brownie and her
colt, Kiki had an idea.
When Stunt Night came there
was Kiki prancing and whinnying just like Brownie.
Kiki was the only camper who could whinny, but
after that all the campers wanted to play horse.

And the next day

Kiki showed them just how
she had made a horse mask
from a brown paper bag.

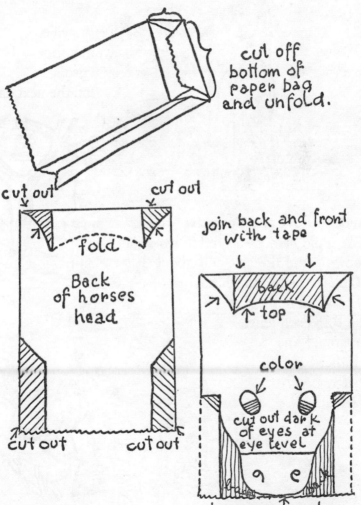

cut off
bottom of
paper bag
and unfold.

cut out   cut out

fold

Back
of horses
head

cut out   cut out

join back and front
with tape

back
top

color

cut out dark
of eyes at
eye level

shape muzzle

Then it was the last day at camp.
Kiki hated to say good-by to Brownie and her colt
but she promised to come back next summer.

And when she and Coco saw Mommy at the station
Kiki could hardly wait to tell her about
Brownie and the colt and about Stunt Night.
"Oh, Mother, I can whinny
just like Brownie. I'm
the BEST whinnier
in camp!" And
Mother thought
that was
wonderful.

A Brown Bear uses weapons to catch his dinner.

Weapons in Nature

Most wild creatures have built-in weapons which help to keep them out of serious trouble. Horns, strong teeth, claws, and poisonous stings are just a few kinds of them. There are even a few fishes which can give other creatures quite an electric shock when they want to!

An animal's weapons are very important to him. He can use them to catch food. Very often, too, they help him defend himself against attack by other creatures. He never has to learn how or when to use them. Even while he is very young he can make them work surprisingly well.

A Brown Bear has two sets of first-rate weapons. One, of course, is his big teeth inside strong jaws. The other is his paws with their long, curved claws. With these he catches

117

many a meal of raw fresh fish by wading right in the water and scooping up a big trout or maybe a salmon. He looks too large and clumsy for this sort of fishing. But he can really move very fast when he wants to.

Several other kinds of bears fish this way during the warm weather. They also use their front feet and claws to rake the ripe fruit from blueberry and other bushes. Fruit is one of their favorite foods. So is the honey which wild bees often store in hollow trees. The bears just rip the tree apart and gobble the honey. Their thick fur is fine protection against the bees' stings while they lick up this sweet meal.

When two wild bears get mad at each other, they sometimes have a real battle. They wrestle, bite and scratch with amazing speed and skill. And when one of them decides that he has had enough, he will take off as fast as a man could run.

The African Lion also uses his great claws and jaws for food-catching as well as self-defense. An old male has a thunderous roar, too, which sometimes frightens other animals almost to death!

The Lion can drag down and kill an animal considerably larger than himself. His strength is tremendous; and much of his hunting is done at night. When he charges an enemy, he can rush forward at a speed of forty miles an hour. But some hunters say that he is not nearly as brave as he pretends to be.

Another of the large wild beasts of Africa is the Rhinoceros. He is much bigger and heavier than a lion, and his thick skin is very tough. There are no claws on his broad feet, but he has a bad temper and is afraid of nothing. He

The African Lion has tremendous claws and jaws.

The Rhinoceros uses his horns only for fighting

sometimes has two great horns on top of his snout, instead of only one. They are not solid, like the horns of a deer, but are made of many long, tough hairs cemented together.

It is a strange fact that the Rhinoceros has such poor eyesight that, when he charges, his enemy can often escape by jumping to one side at the last minute. He uses his horns almost entirely as weapons. They are of little use for gathering food, as their owner eats nothing except parts of plants which cannot fight back!

The Bighorn Sheep also lives on grass and other plants, like our ordinary tame sheep. The males have tremendous curling horns which they use for fighting each other or any other animals foolish enough to attack them. Their method is to lower their heads and charge at top speed. When two of them rush at each other they crash head-on like a couple of runaway locomotives. These smashes can be heard for a

Bighorn Rams lower curled horns when charging.

The powerful Vulture   *The strong Mute Swan*

long distance in our high western mountains where this splendid animal lives.

Many kinds of birds, like the Mute Swan, use their bills mostly for gathering food and also for fighting. This web-footed water bird is pure white except for some black on his wings and face. When he is hungry he pokes his long neck and head under water and grabs submerged plants and any little creatures he can find. His best weapons are his wings, with which he can strike really heavy blows.

The Mute Swan is one of our largest birds. When he flies he is almost five feet long from the tip of his bill to the end of his tail. And his opened wings may spread as much as eight feet.

Vultures use their powerful, hooked beaks for tearing their food into pieces small enough to swallow. They can fight with them, too, if they have to. These huge, homely birds are found in many tropical parts of the world. Their principal food is the flesh of dead animals.

Some of those Jellyfishes which you see along an ocean beach in summer have poisonous streamers which sting anything they touch. This is their way of killing the other much smaller water creatures which are their natural food. Sometimes these stinging tentacles are useful, too, as protection from their enemies. The name "Jellyfish" comes from the jelly-like stuff which forms their bodies.

Another strange creature with much longer tentacles is called Portuguese Man-of-War. This soft-bodied little fish

A Jellyfish to avoid   *Portuguese Man-of-War*

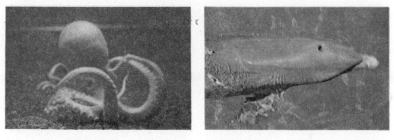

Octopus, a wrestler   *Dolphin strikes with snout.*

really does look somewhat like a tiny ship when it floats along on the surface of warm oceans. His tentacles hang quite a distance down into the water. His poison is strong enough to kill any little fish he touches. Then the Man-of-War eats him. The queer weapons of the Man-of-War and the Jellyfish are painful to people, but not really dangerous.

Deeper in the ocean, and usually where there are large rocks which make good hiding places, is the home of the famous Octopus. His eight long, strong tentacles contain no poison. Instead, all along his under side there are many small suction discs which look like small, shallow saucers. These can get a deadly grip on any creature against which they are pressed. When the Octopus has caught a fish or some other living food with them, his tentacles carry it to his mouth which is near the bottom of the bulb-like body that you see in the photograph.

The Porpoise, or Dolphin, looks somewhat like a fish, but really he is a warm-blooded mammal that lives in the oceans of the world. A big one weighs several hundred pounds and can swim tremendously fast. His weapon is a long snout that is almost as hard as concrete. With this he and his companions can batter a shark so badly that they

123

are able to chew him up with their sharp teeth.

The hundreds of different bees, wasps and hornets use their poisonous, needle-like stingers for defending their home nests and driving off any creature which bothers them. Even horses and cows are sometimes attacked so savagely that they run away as fast as they can.

The females of the bee family are the only ones who have stingers. This is because they are the ones who do all the work and are most likely to need weapons. The males are harmless and lazy. This is why they are called "drones".

The Black Widow Spider is poisonous, too, but in a different way. Instead of injecting the poison with a stinger she uses a pair of sharp curved jaws called mandibles. With these she grabs and kills small insects to eat. Sometimes, in self-defense, she will bite a person who she thinks is threatening her life. Her bite may be really serious.

It is important for everyone interested in animals to understand which weapons of wildlife to avoid close contact with. Remember that any creature will defend himself if threatened—and that most of them are really afraid of *you*.

Paper Wasps sting.

Deadly Black Widow

Factory Kitty

by HELEN HOKE

illustrated by POLLY JACKSON

Everybody remembers the day the kitten came to the RITZ
PRINT AND DYE WORKS.

Tony, the head dyer, is the one who started it all. One
noontime when the whistle blew, he decided it was such
a nice sunny day he would eat his lunch outside. In no time
at all, all the other workers brought their lunches boxes outside, too. And the big yard in front of the factory turned
into a picnic ground.

Text copyright, 1949, by Franklin Watts, Inc.

And then, suddenly, there was the kitten. Perhaps it had smelled the delicious salami that Mrs. Tony had put in Tony's lunch box. Perhaps it just liked picnics. Certainly, it had no way if knowing it had entered the PRIVATE PROPERTY of a big busy noisy factory filled with machines that clattered and giant cutters that slashed through heavy cloth with a dangerous swish, and great vats of boiling hot dye, all colors of the rainbow.

It was a very small kitten and a very sad-looking kitten, with a torn ear and its ribs sticking out. But it was a very brave kitten, standing there in a strange place, facing all the strange men like a fierce little orange-and-yellow-and-black tiger.

"Well, I'll be," said Tony, "if that isn't a regular Calico Cat. My grandmother had one . . . a little tiger of a cat, fierce and proud and full of beans."

"Well *this* one's certainly full of beans." Mike laughed because the kitten had quietly begun to nibble at the nice little pot of beans that Mrs. Mike had put in the lunch box.

"Makes himself at home, doesn't he?" said Jake.

"Sure, makes himself at home out here in the yard, but I'll bet he turns scaredy-cat just like the others when we get him *inside* the factory," Mike said.

But Mike was wrong. After lunch, when they all went back to work, Calico followed right along. He gave one small leap in the air when the machinery began to roar. But that was all. Then he began to explore. Delicately, he picked his way between whizzing wheels and rows of cloth that zoomed up and down on a thing that looked like a roller coaster. He stood with his small head cocked beside

the dye bath and saw yards and yards of material go in grey and come out red. He watched the workmen load the cloth on little trucks to be carried down to the storeroom. He peered into the quiet office where the Big Boss sat at an ordinary desk, but he didn't stay very long.

"Too peaceful for him around here," the Big Boss said.

There was only one place Calico didn't go. That was down in the basement where the goods were stored. The basement belonged to Big Tom, the black cat who had been with the factory for years. Big Tom would not bother with the rest of the factory. The basement—where there was a danger of rats eating the cloth—was his Hunting Ground. And the big barred iron door to the basement was kept carefully closed.

"Wait till tomorrow—Calico won't be here," the Big Boss said when he left that evening. "No kitten has ever stayed for more than a day. But I hope he does—and that he's a good mouser. Big Tom has all he can handle, down-stairs."

"Well, he seems to be settling down for the night," said Tony.

Sure enough, Calico, all by himself, had found an old heap of rags and made himself a bed.

The next morning all the workmen brought something extra in their lunch pails. If that little Calico was still around, he was going to have his reward. And indeed he *was* still around. And what a story the night watchman had to tell!

"That little critter turned up every°hour just as if he knew when I had to punch the time clock. He followed me all over the place. And *mice*—he's a born mouser. Little as he is, he's tough! Had 'em laid out in *rows*. Big Tom didn't even need to inspect, upstairs, last night, when I left the door open for him. Only place Calico *won't* go is down in the storeroom. Reckon Big Tom told him that was Private Property."

Within a week, Calico knew just what he liked to do, every hour. He liked to be in the spot with the most action. At seven o'clock he was in the dye room, where he ate the salami that Tony gave him, drank a saucer of coffee, and then sat quietly studying the colors the men were mixing.

"Blue is his favorite color," Tony said.

"Aw—how do you reckon that?" Jake asked.

"Begins to lick himself and purr whenever we make blue," Tony said.

By noon Calico was hungry again, and after lunch he took a nap. He liked to put his head on an old scrap of blue velvet, as soft as his own kitten's fur.

After his nap, he did his exercises, climbing up and down the ropes and sharpening his claws on them. Sometimes the men gave him a ride in a truck with the goods that were being carried off the floor.

"Look at that, turns his claws in so he won't pull the cloth . . . smart cat," Mike said.

"Smart cat" began to be a phrase that was heard often in the factory. Whoever would suppose, the men said, that a little scrawny kitten could turn into such a daring acrobat!

"Better than a tightrope walker," they said when Calico picked his way daintily along a narrow ledge only half-a-kitten wide.

"Better than a whole circus," they said when Calico did his once-a-day Special Trick. Every day, just before the going-home whistle blew, Calico began his long ride down the newly dyed strip of cloth. It was hot. So he kept dancing

from one foot to another until *just* before the cloth turned
over into the series of steam rollers that dried the wet cloth.
At just that moment, easily—no trouble at all—Calico
leaped across the space between the two banks of steam
rolls, and slid happily down the dry cloth to the heap on
the floor below. It made a first-rate toboggan slide, and the
men watched, every night just before the whistle, to see

Calico do his Special Trick.

He *was* a smart cat all right. He got fooled only once and that was the day that the RITZ PRINT AND DYE WORKS had the big order to print some leopard cloth. When Calico woke up from his nap, the whole factory was filled with leopards. Up and down the roller coaster came the long lengths of material, yellow with black spots . . . furry, moving spots. Calico gave a frightened yelp and began tearing up and down the aisles between the busy machines.

"Silly critter—what's got into him?" Tony asked, shaking his head in bewilderment.

When the Big Boss came walking by just then, he began to laugh. "It's the leopards!" he cried. "Stop the machines."

So for the first time since the electricity failed in a thunderstorm, the machines at the RITZ PRINT AND DYE WORKS were stopped. All because of Calico.

"Now," said the Big Boss, "pick him up, Tony, and show him it's only cloth."

"Reckon you feel pretty silly," Tony said tenderly, as

Calico put out a brave paw and touched the leopard cloth.

And Calico must have felt *very* silly because when the machines began to roar again, he stalked with great dignity back to his bed and pretended to be asleep the rest of the day.

It was the next morning that Calico's love of blue got him into REAL trouble. When he started on his regular inspection of the dye room, there on the floor was a little pan of blue color, as blue as a lake on a summer's day. It was hot in the dye room. And the blue in the pan looked very cool. Suddenly Calico could stand it no longer. He dipped his nose into the cool blue. But it wasn't cool. It was hot. Burning hot. Calico yelped with surprise and misery.

"Jumping Juniper," Tony cried, "get Miss Alice."

Miss Alice sat in the office with the Big Boss. She was the one who fixed the cuts and the burns.

Poor Calico. He had burned his nose. Miss Alice put some salve on it, but Calico kept licking off the salve. And the salve had a horrid taste. Miss Alice finally put a bandage over Calico's nose, to cover the salve.

Calico felt very sick. All day long he lay on his heap of rags with his head on the piece of blue velvet. He was very brave, but occasionally the men heard a faint moan and they knew he was suffering.

When it was time to go home, no one wanted to leave him. Finally the Big Boss himself said: "I think I'd better take him home with me. He's a fine brave little kitten, but this noisy factory is no place for him. Jimmy and Jill, my two young ones, will love him and there is a big green lawn where he can play."

Nobody said a word because the Big Boss was usually right about things. But it was a very sad crowd of men who gathered up their empty lunch boxes and started home.

"Reckon we'll miss Calico a lot," Tony said sadly.

"Yes," said Jake, "and what's more—I reckon Calico'll miss us!"

And Jake was right. At first, things happened so quickly that Calico didn't miss anyone. He was whisked into a big automobile and driven to a big white house on a hill. He saw lots of grass, as green as the beautiful green dye Tony mixed. And blue, blue sky, his favorite shade of blue.

Then, as soon as the Big Boss carried him inside the house, things happened even faster. A pretty little girl took him from the Big Boss's arms and hugged him tight. But the Big Boss said, "You'll have to wait till his nose gets better, Jill. Better put him down now. You can play with him all you want when he's well again."

Calico stood in the middle of a big soft rug and stared

up at Jill. She was a nice little girl, but he was not at all sure he wanted her to hug him. Then a little boy came running up. He was even smaller than the little girl, and right away he reached for Calico's tail.

"No, Jimmy, no!" said his father. "Poor Calico doesn't feel well. You can play with him when he gets better."

Calico stared at Jimmy and sighed. Jimmy looked like a nice little boy, but Calico was not at all sure that he wanted anybody to pull his tail.

A lady in a stiff, starched dress brought him a dish of warm milk. It was very nice milk, but it did not have the flavor of onions or salami or beans. Calico sighed again.

Then the lady said, "Shouldn't we give him a bath? He must have picked up all kinds of germs in the factory."

"Not yet," the Big Boss told her. "He doesn't feel well enough to have a bath yet."

Calico didn't know what the lady meant by "bath," but he felt it was probably not anything very pleasant.

Calico shivered. Everything was so quiet here, and so strange. He felt sure he wasn't going to like it anywhere nearly as much as he did the factory.

Sure enough, Calico didn't like it. The pretty little girl named Jill dressed him up in her doll clothes and took him for a ride in a buggy. Calico was miserable. It was nothing like the rides in a real truck he had had. The little boy Jimmy pulled his tail every chance he got. And that nurse in the stiff, starched clothes spent all her time giving people—and kittens—baths.

Calico got fatter and healthier, and his nose was all well. But he kept on being unhappy. Sometimes he woke up with a start, thinking it was time for him to catch up with the night watchman. Sometimes in his dreams he heard the whir of the machinery and the swish of the giant cutters. But when he woke he heard nothing more exciting than the tinkling chimes of the big clock in the hall.

Then one day Calico saw a big truck outside the door, and the man in the truck was the very same man who had always given him a piece of herring out of his lunch box at the factory. Sure enough, the man was carrying a big bolt of cloth into the house—leopard cloth—the very same yellow cloth with black spots that had scared poor Calico so much.

Calico jumped all the way down to the ground from the second-story window and, before anyone saw him, hopped up into the truck and hid under a big parcel. When the driver came down the walk and got back into the truck, Calico's heart beat fast with excitement. He was with his friends again.

Whizz—grrr went the engine of the truck. *Squeak* went the brakes. And off they went.

After a long ride, the truck stopped and Calico peered out. His heart stopped beating. No factory. No familiar workmen. This was a big building with a roof, but no sides. And there was noise all around, and whistles tooting all the time. Calico saw two silver rails shining in the sun. The next minute a big black engine came roaring along, and the silver rails were hidden by a long row of cars. And now hundreds of people were suddenly on the platform, most

of them carrying suitcases and boxes. Calico began to worry about losing the nice man from the factory who had driven him here in the truck.

Calico scrambled out, looking eagerly for the man who always gave him a piece of herring. But the man had disappeared. Calico knew there was just one thing to do. He must find his friend at once. Like a flash, he streaked across to the platform.

"Get out of here," a strange man said, reaching out with his foot toward Calico. Calico streaked off in another direction. And then, another. His friend wasn't anywhere. And the truck! Where had it gone to? Calico couldn't find it, either.

For days, poor Calico wandered. He found that some people pushed him away; some yelled "S-C-AT!" at him. Life was a weary round of ducking and dodging and keeping one jump ahead of big dogs and ladies with brooms and bad little boys with sling shots. He slept in strange places. And it wasn't long before he had very little to eat.

By this time Calico looked very much the way he had looked that first day at the factory—thin and bedraggled and sad. But he was still a fierce tiger cat at heart. And everywhere he went, he looked for just one thing—his beloved factory where he had so many fine friends.

And then one day he saw a big cat eating a piece of fish. The fish looked delicious. And it smelled very much like the herring from the lunch box at the factory. Calico was hungry. He was much smaller than the big cat, but he was willing to fight for just one taste of that fish.

At first, the big cat did not even bother to fight. He just brushed Calico away with his paw. But when Calico nipped the big cat from behind, the big cat snarled. And in a minute the fur began to fly!

"Just one bite of that fish," thought Calico. "I don't care if I do lose an ear trying to get it."

"Oh," screamed a lady in a big automobile parked at the curb, nearby. "Oh, oh!"

And the next thing Calico knew, the lady had come to his rescue.

She waved her umbrella at the big cat.

"Brute," she cried angrily at the big cat, "what do you mean, trying to steal from this little kitty?"

Lickety-split, the big cat ran, and Calico gulped down the fish. It was even more delicious than he had thought it would be. But he was not so happy when the lady picked him up and carried him into her automobile. He already knew that he didn't like trucks that took him to strange places. So, when the engine started up and went *whizz—grrr*, just like the truck, even though there wasn't any squeak, Calico was very much upset.

Then in a little while, there he was in another strange place. It was an apartment house, and he had to ride in an elevator to get up to the tenth floor, where the lady lived. Calico didn't like her apartment at all. It had too many things in it. He wanted to get out. But when he ran over to the window in the living room, he saw it was much too high to jump down from.

Even though he had plenty to eat, Calico was unhappy. The lady, who was called Miss Muff, patted him too much. Every day she took him for a ride. And whenever she took him for a walk, she put a leather thing around his neck so he couldn't run away. That was even worse than being dressed in doll clothes! Every day, Calico felt more and more bored.

Then a wonderful thing happened. It happened one day when Miss Muff took him for his daily ride. When Miss Muff did that, she never bothered to put the leather thing around his neck. Calico always sat beside her on the front seat on a fat satin pillow, looking wistfully out of the window. Miss Muff thought he was having a good

time. But he wasn't having a good time.

Now on this particular day, Miss Muff was driving along when all of a sudden there was a big bang and the car stopped.

"Oh, dear," said Miss Muff. "A blowout. A real blowout. What shall I do?"

"There's a garage about two blocks back, ma'am," a man on the sidewalk said. "Walk down there and they'll send someone back to fix your tire."

"Oh, thank you," said Miss Muff. She was so excited about the tire she forgot all about the open window beside her. She almost forgot Calico—but not quite. "Be a good boy, kitty," she called back as she got out of the car and hurried away.

No sooner had Miss Muff disappeared around the corner, than with one flying leap Calico was out of the window and streaking away in the opposite direction. All day long he ran and ran and ran. He hid in alleys and behind bushes, and he wandered for miles and miles.

When at last it was night and the dark was all around him, Calico went more and more slowly. It was a very hot night, and he began to wish he could find some cool water. He suddenly remembered that it had been a long time—hours and hours—since he had had a drink of water. He remembered about all the nice cool water at the factory. Oh, to be back at the factory!

Slowly, Calico kept on walking. And after a while he smelled a faint fishy smell. Following the smell, he came to a little canal. The moonlight made stripes of gold on the water. The little canal looked familiar. Was it? Yes, it was! Suddenly he saw a big building rising out of the shadows. It looked almost like . . . . it *was* . . . the factory itself! Calico started to run, then stopped in his tracks. For along the canal, a black slow-moving shape came stalking. It was Big Tom out for a walk. Calico slid back into the shadows and watched.

Big Tom stepped slowly along the canal. He seemed to be looking for something in the water. And then, quick as a flash, his paw darted into the water and out it came with something shiny.

"A fish! He's caught a fish," thought Calico.

Big Tom ate the fish and then walked on, once more. He was coming nearer and nearer, and Calico felt his heart beat faster. In the factory, Big Tom had never hurt him.

Big Tom had just paid no attention to him at all. Big Tom had merely acted as if Calico didn't belong to the factory. But what would he do now if he saw Calico trying to get into the factory?

Then and there Calico made up his mind. He wasn't going to let Big Tom or anything else scare him away. Now that he had found the factory again, he intended to stay there. So he stepped bravely out into the moonlight where Big Tom could see him.

Big Tom stopped walking. For a long time, he stared at Calico, then came closer and closer. Calico stood still and stared back. After a long time, Big Tom did a most surprising thing. He turned and walked back to the canal. In a second, flash went his paw, and out came another fish. Then Big Tom brought the fish back to where Calico was standing and dropped it in front of him. Would Big Tom fight for the fish? Suddenly, Calico knew he was so hungry he didn't care. Thrusting out his paw, he pulled the fish toward him and started gobbling it down. He ate it all. And Big Tom didn't even growl. He simply stood and watched, then turned around and went back to the canal.

Calico waited a minute. "Well!" thought Calico. "Well!" and he knew at once that this was his chance. And quick as a wink, there he was, streaking off toward the factory.

Next morning, what a story the night watchman had to tell Tony and Jake and all the others!

"There he was, smiling, if you please, standing by the time clock when I came to ring in. First he showed me the mice he had caught—lots and lots of mice. Then he went to my lunch box for something to eat. Then he went right over to that old heap of rags and fussed around until he found his special piece of blue velvet, curled up and went off to sleep. Just too tired to follow me around and help me punch the time clock."

"Told you he could take care of himself," said Tony. "Wonder where he went when he ran away from the Big Boss. He looks pretty well fed."

"Anyway, he got back—so who cares where he went," said Jake.

"Do you suppose the Big Boss will want to take him

home again?" Mike asked in a worried voice, as the Big Boss came out of his office.

Calico woke up, stretched himself, and began to purr so loudly that the men were sure he understood what the Big Boss said to Mike then, "Take him home? No, I don't think so. He's a Career Kitty at heart, that's exactly what he is. It's on the job for him from now on!"

bbbrr-BBBBRRRRRR went the machines as the factory day began and the work got under way. *purr*RRRRR went Calico happily, head cocked and four feet poised for a flying leap into the big room full of noise and action. He was on the job and so was everyone else—and they were all much too busy to see Old Tom peering around the corner of the basement door with what might almost have been a grin on his battered old face.

The Fairy
and the Doll

A LITTLE PLAY FOR CHILDREN

by ROSE FYLEMAN

illustrated by PHYLLIS ROWAND

★ · · · ★ · · · ★

CHARACTERS

SILVERWING, a fairy
PATTY'S DOLL *The doll should speak in a squeaky voice.*

SCENE

A Garden.

The DOLL *is lying flat on her face on the ground with arms and legs stretched out.*

Enter SILVERWING.

SILVERWING.
Why, here's Patty's doll, left to spend the night in the garden. Oh, cruel Patty! Get up, my dear, you'll get stiff if you lie there all night.

DOLL.
I can't. I'm a doll. Dolls can't.

SILVERWING.

Oh, I forgot. I'll soon make that all right.

She circles round the DOLL *, waving her wand, and touches the doll on legs and arms. Each time she touches her the* DOLL *gives a little jerk.*

SILVERWING.

Tilly, tally, tolly, tell,
I will weave a magic spell.
Tippy, tappy, toppy, tup,
Now you'll find you can get up.

DOLL, *sitting up and still speaking in a squeaky voice.*
Who are you?

SILVERWING.
I'm a fairy.

DOLL.
Oh! Where do you live?

SILVERWING.
I'm living in the lilac tree at the corner of the lawn just now.
But I shall move next month. The lilac's nearly over.

DOLL.
It must be pretty to live in a tree.

SILVERWING.
Yes. Better than being knocked about in a nursery. I wonder you stand it.

DOLL

It's not very nice sometimes. Patty does forget so. She leaves me in the most dreadful places.

SILVERWING.
It's a great shame.

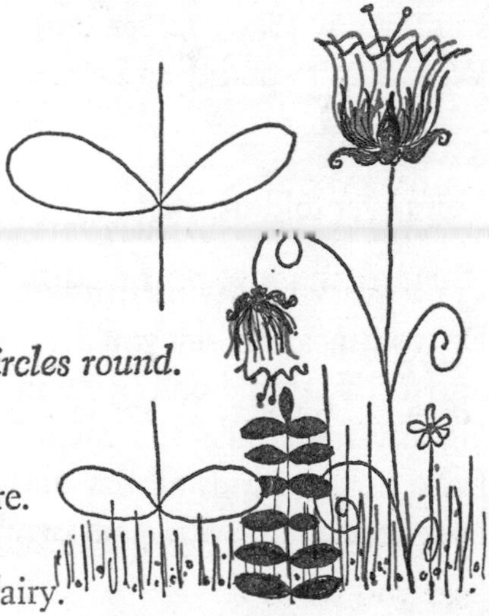

Pause.

I know what I'll do.

Waves wand and again circles round.

Jeery, jary, jiry, jore,
You shall be a doll no more.
Leery, lory, liry, lary,
You are changed into a fairy.

The DOLL *gets up and moves lightly about. She waves her arms and dances a few steps.*

DOLL.
Oh, how lovely! How pleased Patty will be to have a real live doll.

SILVERWING.
Oh, but you can't go back to Patty. That would never do. You're a fairy now and you must come and live in Fairyland. Besides, I'm sure you don't want to be a doll again. Patty wasn't a bit nice to you, you know.

DOLL.
Oh yes, she was. Only careless. You see, she loves me very much. I'm afraid I couldn't leave Patty.

SILVERWING, *rather cross.*
Why didn't you say so before?

DOLL.
You never told me that . . .

SILVERWING, *interrupting.*
Do you mean to say you'd rather be changed back again into a stiff, stupid doll living in the nursery and never having any fun, when you might be a fairy, and dance and frolic in the woods all day and sleep on the swaying lilac boughs at night with stars twinkling at you?

DOLL.
It sounds very nice. But . . .

shaking her head

I can't leave Patty.

SILVERWING, *crossly.*
Oh, very well. If you won't, you won't.

Same business.

Toffy, taffy, teffy, tiff,
Arms and legs again are stiff.
Tilly, tally, tully, toll,
Change again into a doll.

DOLL *falls back onto the ground:*

SILVERWING, *looking at her.*
You *are* a funny creature, you know. But I think it's rather
sweet of you to stick to Patty. I'll tell the Fairy King to see
that you don't take any harm. Good-bye.

DOLL, *squeakily.*
Good-bye!

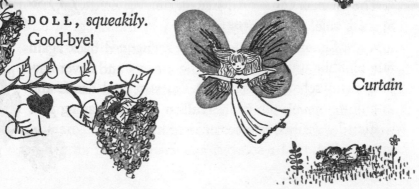

Curtain

Let's Visit Ecuador

Ecuador is a small country on the western coast of South America. It is called Ecuador, which means equator in Spanish, because the equator runs across the country. This tiny land is full of scenic contrasts: hot lowlands along the Pacific coast, highlands crowned with snow-capped old volcanoes, and the rain-soaked Amazon jungle. Though Ecuador is in the tropics, the climate is cool because most of the country lies high in the Andes Mountains.

Ecuador is a poor country. It must depend on imports for its metals and machinery, and some of its food and textiles. It produces only agricultural products like bananas, coffee, cocoa, rice, tropical fruits, and nuts to sell to other nations. These crops grow in the coastal lowlands.

Most Ecuadorians live in the picturesque valleys and basins of the Andean highlands. Here they farm and raise livestock. Beyond the mountains, the dense green jungle begins. Wandering Indian tribes live there—some of them wild tribes like the Jivaros, savage head-hunters who still use poison blowguns to kill animals and men!

The Spanish conquered Ecuador in 1534. After years of Spanish rule, the country was freed by the forces of revolutionist Simon Bolivar. Complete independence as a separate republic was achieved in 1830. Since then, there have been many rebellions, sometimes caused by the differences in culture among the white, Indian, and Negro people.

Ecuador's future sources of wealth lie in her agriculture, untapped mineral resources, and many tourist attractions.

The Flag of Ecuador

In the Ambato market, poor people buy sleeping mats made of straw or rushes.

Colorado Indians paint their bodies with vegetable wax.

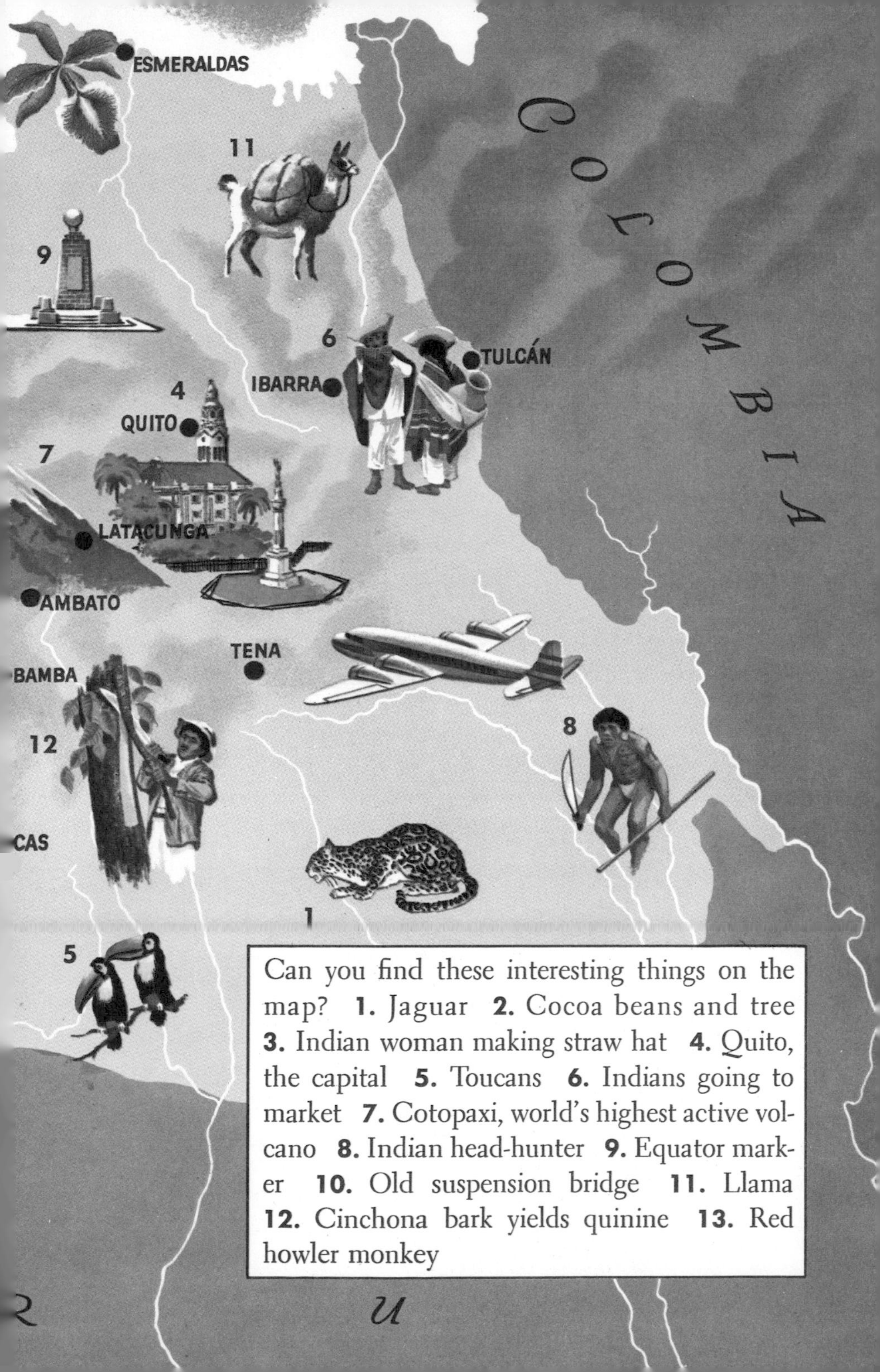

ESMERALDAS

11

9

6

TULCÁN

IBARRA

4

QUITO

7

LATACUNGA

AMBATO

TENA

BAMBA

12

8

CAS

1

5

C O L O M B I A

Can you find these interesting things on the map? **1.** Jaguar **2.** Cocoa beans and tree **3.** Indian woman making straw hat **4.** Quito, the capital **5.** Toucans **6.** Indians going to market **7.** Cotopaxi, world's highest active volcano **8.** Indian head-hunter **9.** Equator marker **10.** Old suspension bridge **11.** Llama **12.** Cinchona bark yields quinine **13.** Red howler monkey

Beautiful Chimborazo, Ecuador's highest inactive volcano.

Shaky old bridges still cross deep ravines and streams.

Sure-footed llamas carry heavy packs in the mountains.

Printed in the United States of America